# OFF LIMITS

# Also by Darlena Taylor-Bonds

Hidden Thoughts

A Woman In The Body Of A Child

Red Balloon

My Southern Roots: Statesville To Detroit

Darlena Taylor-Bonds

OFF LIMITS

Taylor-Bonds Books©2007

Taylor-Bonds Books

First Printing, May 2007

OFF LIMITS/Darlena Taylor-Bonds
ISBN 978-0-6151-5602-6

OFF LIMITS

# Introduction

## Karma

Philosophy according to which the quality of peoples current and future life is determined by their behavior in this life.

What are you in stored for? This is all be determined by what you give out, meaning what you do, it will surely come back to you.

# Characters

Gail Halsey               Gary Halsey

David Knight              Sabrina Knight

Michelle Peterson         Josh Strong

Scott - Bully drug dealer    Robert-crack addict

Bruce-Bar Patron

Dedication


This book is dedicated to all those people who have experienced infidelity within their life. Do not let it change the person that you are, keep your head held high and keep walking. For it is not you that had the problem.

I get tired of men and women who will knowingly be involved with married people, but try to take advantage of the so-called benefits they receive. I do not excuse the cheating spouse of any wrongdoing, because they are the one's that is breaking their vows. However, the man or woman who knowingly date married people do not get off the hook so easily either. Our moral fiber of society over the years has been shredded into pieces. The cheaters should be held responsible for their role in destroying marriages and families. Although the common statement made is "it takes two to tango", so why shouldn't both be held responsible to share the blame and shame?

Maybe you are enticed by the "thrill" of sneaking around or living "dangerously". Then you should consider what type of person you are. "Scary thought isn't it?" Are you so desperate, you will take whatever attention you can get? Maybe you knew that girlfriend or boyfriend was married and knowing it, your knowledge intensified your twisted attraction and made you get involved. So sad and scary that you would share someone just to get your adrenaline pumping. Maybe you are that closet person, but if things do not go your way, you want to call the spouse and tell.

Did you ever consider making that call and say, "Hey, I'm fucking your spouse, when you found out they were married in the beginning?" In your mind you have convinced yourself he or she love you so much until they are going to leave their family for you. Allowing the both of you to ride into happily ever after. Please wake up! Why would you think that if a man or woman would cheat and break up his or her family, would really care about you? Even if he or she did leave their family, could they be faithful to you? You are fooling yourself if you think this is possible. It is different if you did not know about their family or spouse at home, but you do. You know but do not care. You do not care about yourself or the innocent children that is being hurt by your selfish and disgusting behavior. In addition, if you make that call to their spouse, you really were stooping low. Have you ever called, insulted or harassed the spouse?

Then you are justifying your jealously misdirected anger on the innocent spouse, who has not done anything wrong in this sticky mess.

How do you accept that Mr. or Mrs. Lover telling you "their marriage had been over for a while now but he or she still lives in the house?" In addition, you tell yourself that the spouse "deserves" to be cheated on for being stupid and didn't leave? You are not a "fool for not knowing, you are a fool when you know and do nothing about it". No matter what that lover say to you, you are an adult and should be able to decide for yourself what is right or wrong. Why settle for part time visits or meetings whenever they can sneak away. Are you satisfied with someone who cannot spend major holidays with you? Alternatively, is saying, "I love you" to someone else? Even if you do not care about hurting the children or helping tear a family apart, have some respect for yourself...

## Fool's Way of Thinking

Gail Halsey, the typical homemaker that has everything she wanted. A lovable husband Gary that worked long hard hours at the plant, bringing her home his paid check to care for the household.

Gary was not the type of man that ran the streets or went out to party on the weekend. All he did was work and came home. They enjoy the company of their long time friends, David and Sabrina Knight.

The couples would get together periodically to play cards, drink and have fun on the weekends and some holidays.

Now Gary has another friend, Josh Strong that work at the same plant as he does. Gail younger sister, Michelle comes over to their house on a regular basis, talking to Gail about all the men that she been dating.

This particular day while Gary was working Michelle came over and asked Gail "why don't you go out with me this weekend and have some fun?"

All you do is sit in this house and play molly house cleaner, how do you know that Gary is not tipping on you? Gail responded "look girl don't come in here with that dumb ass shit about my husband cheating ok?"

Michelle's only rebuttal was "ah girl if he told you it was raining and you saw his penis in his hand, you would believe it"

"So damn naïve" was what Michelle said as she walks out the door. Michelle did not have children or a husband so she was what society seen as a "loose woman"

Michelle stuck her head slightly back in the door "hey but consider going ok?" then she walked to her car and sped out the driveway.

"That crazy ass Michelle" she never quit was what Gail thought as she continued to fix Gary's dinner. Gail and Sabrina had a relationship that if Gail wanted to know about something, she always called Sabrina and talk to her about it.

It was no hold barred with the two of them, Sabrina on the other hand was an undercover whore; this side of her Gail did know about but trusted her like a sister.

Whenever they talked on the phone Sabrina would always tell Gail "all you need is some dick and everything will be alright"

Gail was so use to Sabrina talking like this until she never paid it any mind just laughed at her and continued talking about whatever they were. Gary was the only man that Gail had ever had sex with and she was very naive to the streets. Sabrina had several men before finally marrying David.

David knew she was not a virgin when they married, but hell, he was a freak himself. David met Sabrina one night while he and his other friends were hanging out at the club.

Sabrina was an exotic dancer at the club and David would come in every Friday after work, what he calls his "happy hour"

Sabrina saw David sitting at the edge of the stage and would always walk over to him, turn and bend her ass over to shake it in his face. David spent good money in the club so all the other dancers would pick him out of the crowd whenever he came in.

This made David feel like he was a celebrity, but the girls didn't care all they want was what he was giving out "his money" Some of the girls would come into the dressing room and swear that he was in the club strictly to see them.

However, strangely he always asked about Sabrina if he did not see her walking around. The club had strict rules that allowed the girls to do lap dances but there wasn't suppose to be no touching from the men, but as everyone knew that there were always men that would find out a way to touch.

The first lap dance David got from Sabrina he told her that he was going to "take her out of the club scene" Sabrina really did not take this serious she thought what he saying was just talk because she knew her movement on his lap got him excited.

Sabrina and Gail grew up and went to school together, besides this they really did not have much in common. Gail was not the outgoing type but Sabrina was, speaking up to anybody and about anything.

Up until Gary married Gail, he used to go to the club with David and the other guys. He just never been in the club that Sabrina worked at. Nevertheless, he has his share of clubbing under his belt.

Although the couples get together now, initially the first time they all met David accused Gary of looking at Sabrina in a way that was not appropriate to him.

David never confronted Gary about it, but did tell Sabrina when they got home that he saw Gary looking at her in a way that he did not like.

Sabrina told David that he was making it all up in his mind and that she knew Gary was happily married to Gail. David still insisted he is still a man, and a man will look if he thought that he had a chance to get what he was looking at.

Even if he could not have it then he could at least imagine. Sabrina did not pay it any mind and continued to walk around the house ignoring him. She went to their bedroom begun taking her clothes off so that she could take a shower.

David followed close behind, still trying to talk about what he thought he saw Gary doing. Gail was so trustworthy of Sabrina until if David told her about his uncomfortable feeling he had with Gary and Sabrina, she most likely would turn against him never to speak to him again.

Gail was so naïve when it came down to Sabrina, Sabrina could do whatever she wanted to Gail, and Gail would accept it.

When Sabrina got up the next morning and went to the club, she was so egotistical until she could not wait to tell the girls how jealous her man was.

She just knew she was all that and some; she sat at the mirror while putting on her make-up and told the story about what David said about Gary to them.

Some of the girls that did not like Sabrina because of her selfish ways just turned and walked out.

The girls that did not like her at the club would sit and talk behind her back about how she thought that she was "the best bitch here" and if any of the girls heard it that did like her, knew not to tell her because Sabrina was ignorant as hell.

Sabrina once hit a girl over the head with a beer bottle because she thought the girl looked at her funny. Her excuse was "why is the bitch staring at me like that" got up with her beer in her hand then hit the girl with it.

Throughout school, Gail took to Sabrina because Gail did not have anyone to defend her in fights, but Sabrina liking trouble would get involved just to fight.

When she first met Gail, she jumped in her fight just so she could bully the other girl Gail was fighting.

The two of them been friends since that. Michelle, Gail sister was all mouth and would not burst grapes if it were a fruit fight. She could get some shit started but you would have to find her after it did.

Sabrina and Gail would be the one that was left fighting after the shit jumped off, Michele would be long gone. Seem like they would have figured this out but Sabrina did not care as long as she was involved in the fight.

Sabrina did not care who got it started, she was there to finish it.

Back at the club, Sabrina walked on stage and did her usual routine. First grabbing the pole then sliding around it, upside down and shaking her ass.

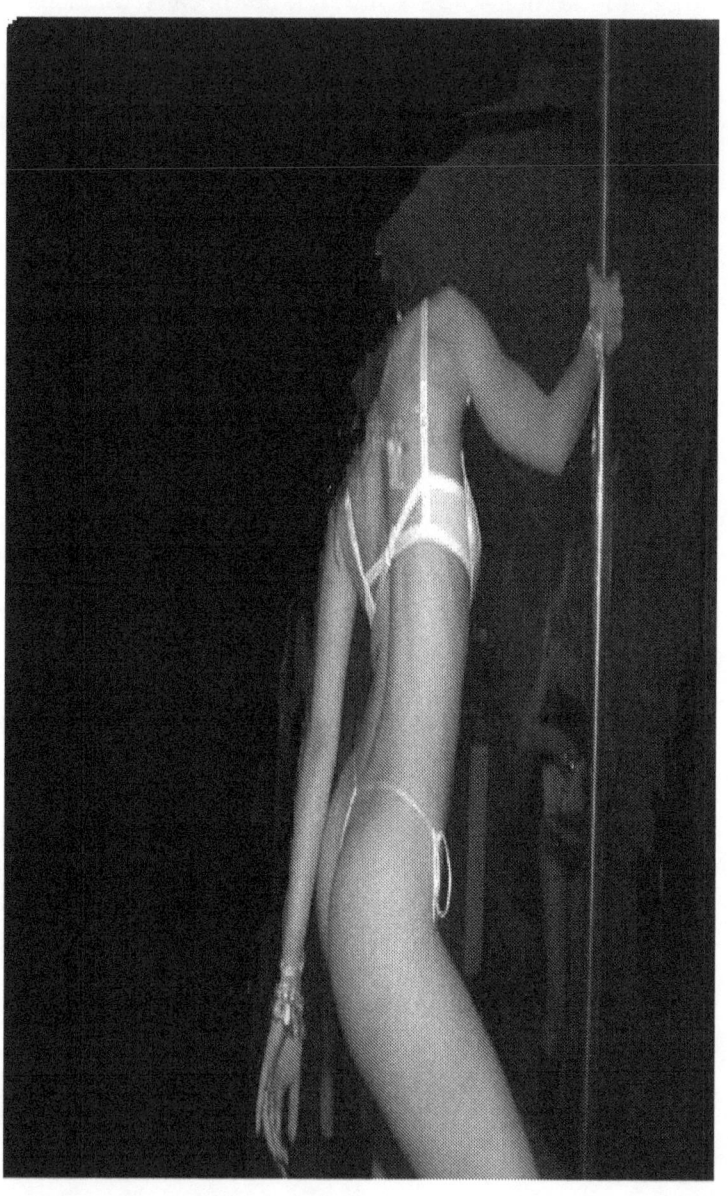

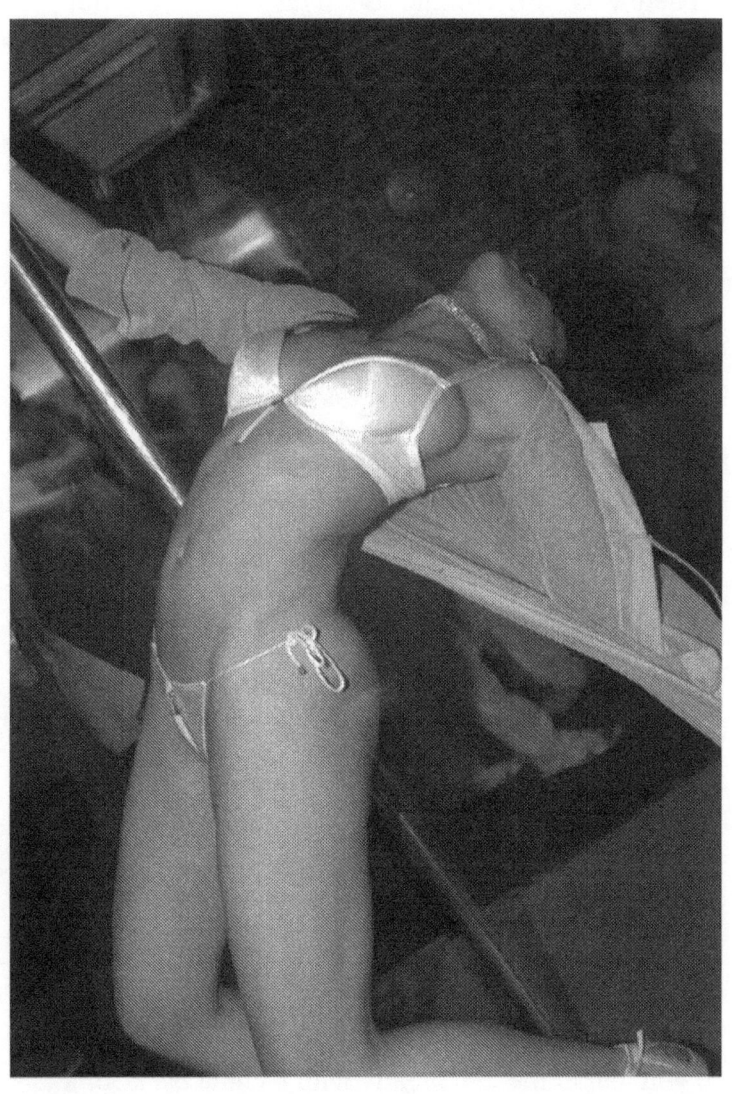

What she said, "she does best" The men sat at the edge of the stage looking with shear delight in their eyes.

There was a big commotion in the back of the club; Sabrina could not see what was going on from the stage due to the lights in her face. She continued to bend down and let the men put their money into her g-string.

After her set, she went into the dressing room to see if anybody knew what the noise was. One of the dancer's involved said "Management was throwing some guy out because he had his dick in his hand while she was trying to give him a lap dance"

The way Sabrina saw this was "the man was the dumb ass; he should have put his shit back in his pants before the management saw him" Sabrina said "fuck that no touching rule, they wouldn't caught me to throw me out if I was me"

The other girl dancers' just laughed at what she said, because it was funny as hell. At the end of the day, Sabrina while driving home called Gail from her cell phone. "What's up, girl?" Sabrina asked as Gail said hello on the other end of the phone.

Gail's reply was "nothing, same old thing just a different day". Sabrina asked "so what you doing today?" Gail replied "getting fucked" They both laughed because Gail usually wasn't the one to talk like this, but this time Gail had beat Sabrina to the punch.

Sabrina told Gail "You are so damn silly" Gail replied, "you taught me to be ready with a come back for a mutha fucker"

Since Gail was hanging around Sabrina, she too knew how to get ignorant at any giving time.

She just chose to carry herself like a woman, but she knew how to get down and dirty.

Sabrina was flamboyant about herself but not Gail, she was sneaky with her shit. Gail did her shit in the closet; even Sabrina did not know this about her.

Although Sabrina told Gail all the stuff about her, Gail never volunteers anything about herself to Sabrina.

Gail knew how to use what information she could get about a person to her advantage, but no one could even do this to her because she was not telling them nothing.

Hey, she felt "if they wanted to tell her their business" that is their problem not hers but she would be willing to listen to it. As Sabrina drove home she turned on the radio, she found the song she liked was on.

She started snapping her fingers, not too much focusing on the road and out of nowhere from how described it was a car in front of her.

"Bam" goes the collision that she caused by not watching where she going. Sabrina's car had glass flying everywhere. The adrenalin if measured now would be off the scale.

Sabrina jump out the car while it appeared in motion, twisting her ankle. Other than her ankle, no one was seriously hurt.

While hobbling to the other driver's car the first thing that she saw was this the old woman that appeared to be her early seventy's. The old woman said "Why didn't you stop at the flashing light?" Sabrina thoughts at that moment was "this old ass lady is literally trying to blame me for what just occurred"

Sabrina did not consider the age of the woman; she jumped in her face and asks "Why did you run the light?" The elderly woman got frightened by Sabrina shaking answered "but you had a red flashing light, mine is yellow"

Sabrina hobbled back to her car to look for her cell phone to call 911. Sabrina opened the car door and sat down. She then began looking around the car for the phone. When she and the woman crashed, her phone obviously fell on the floor of the car somewhere.

Sabrina felt around on the floor and found the phone under the car seat. She dialed 911, the woman on the phone asked "Where's the problem?"

 Sabrina begins to explain what just happened and the operator asked if anyone was hurt or needed an ambulance?

Sabrina told her that beside her ankle hurting that no one else was hurt. The police arrived first then the ambulance came. Sabrina was still sitting inside her car when they arrived.

One ambulance technician came to Sabrina's car and the other went to the elderly woman. The police was busy trying to ask questions to find out what happened and who was at fault. After the technicians loaded Sabrina into the ambulance, one of the police came to the back door and gave Sabrina a ticket for failing to stop at a red light.

Sabrina now was furious; on top of her car being damaged and getting hurt, she gets a ticket. Sabrina was in so much pain at the point until she did not make a big deal about the ticket.

Since Sabrina's car was not damage to the point that it

was not drivable, she told the police that she would have it towed later.

At the hospital, Sabrina's ankle was throbbing with pain. Her ankle was slightly discolored and she could feel the tightness around it.

Sabrina called David but was unable to contact him. Therefore, she called Gail to tell her that she was involve in an accident, but explained that she is ok and she was at the hospital.

Gail told Sabrina that she would continue to try to contact David and she would be right to the hospital.

Gail went to the hospital right away because Sabrina did say that she was ok but Gail did not think she was, she had to see for herself.

 From Gail's point of view, Sabrina could have just said it so Gail did not worry while she was driving to her. Gail arrived at the hospital, parked her car and damn near ran people over going through the entrance doors.

Once inside she walked to the information desk to ask for Sabrina, the woman sitting behind the desk had an "I did not want to work today" look on her face.

Risking It All

Gail asked the woman if Sabrina Knight was transferred into the emergency room today by ambulance. The woman asked Gail who are you may I ask? "I'm her friend" Gail respond.

"Well friend" then you should know if she is here was what the woman said as she turns to look at the computer. Gail asked the woman "what did you just say to me?" the woman did not respond.

Gail just waited patiently without making a big deal out of the woman's sarcastic remark. Finally, after typing into the computer the woman looked at Gail and said yes she is here but she has not been seen by the doctor.

I will tell the patient representative when she can have visitors to let you know. So sign your name on the board over there. As she pointed across the room at a board on the table.

Gail signed her name but the board had so many names on it Gail knew that she would have a wait before she could go to the back to see Sabrina. After waiting about a hour a man came from the back picked up the board and begun calling names "Gail Halsey"

Gail got up a started walking towards the man, he then turned away as he said please follow me. Gail's' thought's were "damn hopefully Sabrina don't have to stay in this hospital because everyone that she had contact with so far was very rude"

The man walk Gail to the back and they get in spot 10, the curtain was partially pulled shut. The representative ask "May we come in?" the worker said sure, this guy was polite.

Gail walked behind the curtain and there she was, Sabrina with her leg propped on top of a pillow. The man was in the middle of wrapping a cast on Sabrina leg. Sabrina had broken her ankle.

Gail laughed and said "My thoughts were right" Sabrina said "what you mean your thoughts were right?" Gail said, "Before I got here I knew you were hurt, but you didn't want me to know how badly"

Sabrina said "Girl you are crazy, when I called you I didn't know it was broke" hell at the accident I was walking on it. I guess my adrenalin was pumping and when I settled down is when I felt the pain.

Do you believe this shit? How can I work like this? Sabrina blurted out while pointing to her leg. Gail said "Sabrina everything happens for a reason, maybe now you can rest the pussy" Sabrina laughed and Gail knew she just said it to cheer Sabrina up to take her mind away from her leg for the moment.

Gail continued to say to Sabrina "I can just see you on stage with that cast on, bend over telling the men to put the money in the cast. They both had to laugh. Gail waited until the hospital discharged Sabrina to drive her home.

On the way to Sabrina's house she and Gail were talking and Sabrina said she was wondering why she could not get I touch with David. As they got to her house David's car was in their driveway, she walked in the house and David was asleep on the couch.

He woke up as they walked into the living room. Still half-asleep David rubbing his eyes said "hey, Sabrina what are you two up to?

Sabrina told David how she was in an accident as if he did not notice her leg in the cast. He said that was my next question "what was with the cast?" Almost like he do not have his priorities straight, that should have been his first question.

She goes on to tell him how she called him and could not get in touch with him, so Gail came and picked her up. Now fully awake David ask her so what happened? How were you involved with the accident?

Sabrina to ashamed to tell David what happened, but she did because she had the ticket and that made it obvious she was at fault.

Even if she changed the subject David was a persistence man, he would not let her get off that easy without asking her again until he got his answer. That's one thing if nothing else women knew about men, if she didn't want him to know something she could change the subject and nine times out of ten he would forget the question before he got his answer.

In a man's mind if the question was not asked twice, then it did not exist. Alternatively, she could play the game he does, change the subject or get angry if he is persistence.

This will make him leave her alone. At least for David this tactic always worked, or he did not care one way or another. In addition, left the question unanswered.
The weather is nice and this weekend the couples decided since Sabrina is in a leg cast, they should go to the park for a barbeque.

The barbeque will be a good idea for Sabrina to allow her to get out the house while enjoying the sun.

The plan was Sabrina could just sit down and let the others do the cooking for her. The group of them knew that Gary had the best damn barbeque in the neighborhood. It was settled they would go early to the park and find an area where they would set-up the grill.

The morning of the barbeque Gary and Gail packed the car for the barbeque. David and Sabrina will buy the meat and other food. Gary and Gail would buy the charcoal and drinks.

This time Gary's friend Josh was invited and everyone knew that Michelle would just invite herself; she did not need any invite. She would come whether they invited her or not. An additive to coming was she knew that Josh would be there.

Josh as Michelle was single and flirty, he would holler at the moon if it were giving pussy away. He just came around on occasions that he thought Michelle would be visiting.

Even if Josh didn't like what he saw in a girl his saying was "pussy don't have a face and dick don't have a conscious"

Although the guy's would laugh at this, they also told him " one day that dick my friend, is going to fall in the toilet when you pull it out to take a piss" his rebuttal always was " I hope the girl can give good head because I'm not fucking her but she can suck me off "

As men do, they would laugh at him and say things like "you're a fool" but that did not stop Josh, he meant what he said. He was looking for any girl that was willing to give him a blowjob. Michelle called Gail that morning just to confirm if Josh was coming she told

Gail "I had to make sure so I would know, if I wanted to put on panties or not"

Gail told her "TMI" too much information. Michelle laughed and told her "aww girl stop acting like a virgin, hell you fuck too"

Gail said "yeah my husband" but Michelle with her smart ass mouth had to say "yeah but who else is he fucking?" Gail then told her "here you go again with that off the wall bull shit" I will talk to you later and hung up the phone.

Gail did not want to hear what Michelle was talking because Michelle always talk like that. Gail was used to hearing Michelle talk about Gary cheating. Gail never had a problem with Gary being unfaithful so why worry about the possibilities of it happening if he never had before.

At the park Sabrina and David arrived first, David found an area where they could set up their grill. Sabrina sat at the table and she was able to work around the table but because of the cast on her leg she did not want to be walking around.

David got the fire started on the grill while waiting for the rest of the group to come. Josh came next; he asked where Gail and David were? He really wanted to know where Michelle was but he knew if Gail were around then Michelle would not be far behind.

He just did not want to make it obvious about his plans that he had in mind for Michelle. Across the park you could see the parking lot; they saw when Gary and Gail arrived. When Gail and Gary pulled up in the car, they were looking around to see if they could see Sabrina or David. Sabrina started waving her arms in the air so they could find where everybody was. Gail was the first out the car; she walked to the back of the car to unload the trunk where they had everything.

Gary got out the car; he then walked around to the trunk to help carry the bags for Gail. Gary took an arm full of bags and begun walking toward the table. Gail was still fumbling around at the car making sure they did not leave anything.

Gary got closer to the table; he saw Sabrina was sitting alone because David was at the grill with Josh stirring the charcoal to make sure that the fire was nice and hot. Gary approached the table across from where Sabrina was sitting.

He begins sitting the bags on the table when Sabrina said "What's going on, Gary?" He responded "Not much how's the leg?" Sabrina talking in a whisper said "the leg would be better if you were between them" while she looked over his shoulder to make sure David could not hear her.

This sort of surprised Gary but he did not want David to know, so he just smiled and said "girl you are so damn crazy" Gail by this time was coming and Sabrina acted as nothing was said. Gary was walking away from the table as Gail was approaching it.

Gary walked over to the grill and he, Josh and David did the man-to-man handshake. David was excited to see Gary but little did he know what just took place at the table. Gail sat down across from Sabrina and asked her "so how's it going girl?"

Sabrina was like a snake; here she was just inviting Gary between her legs but sat looking directly in Gail face as if nothing happened. Sabrina replied to Gail, "It's the same old shit with this leg" Gary never told David what Sabrina said but now knew he can have Sabrina if he wanted her.

Sabrina knew all the time that Gary used to look at her just as David was telling her at the house but wanted to play the game of cat and mouse with Gary. She wanted Gary as bad as he wanted her, but she had to play the role so it would stay undercover.

Gail was supposed to be her friend but Sabrina wanted to fuck her husband, Sabrina could not make it obvious. Not only would Gail be angry with Sabrina, she probably would kick her ass. Gail and Sabrina knew each other since they were kids before they knew what a man was.

Sabrina did not know Gary well enough to risk their friendship over but she just wanted some of the so-called luxuries Gary provider to Gail. She would always tell Gail how lucky she was to have a man like Gary, but Gail never took heed to what Sabrina was saying. As her friend, Gail thought Sabrina was complimenting her on her marriage and household.

Little did Gail know Sabrina wanted what she had, Gary? Gail trusted Sabrina enough to tell her about how Gary made love to her. This only enticed Sabrina's curiosities, making her wonder what he would be like with her. Of course, Sabrina never told Gail but Sabrina had her own idea on how she would go after Gary behind Gail's back. David, although married to Sabrina would only serve as a mean so he could help her get around Gary more.

Besides the fact that their wives grew up together, David and Gary were good friends that is why the two of them were so close. Michelle was not with Gail and Gary when they got to the park, she wanted to make her own entrance on the scene so Josh could have "all eyes on her" Michelle did arrive and she had on practically nothing.

Her shorts were so short until they fit into the folds of the bottom of her ass cheeks. The halter she was wearing consisted of just one piece of material and the strings that held it up. All her back was exposed; her sandals had tie string that wrapped around her legs.

She did make her grand appearance and not only was Josh looking but she got some of the other people attention that was at the park too. The women looking did not said much but if she could read their minds I am sure she would not like what it was saying.

As Michelle approached the table Gail asked "Michelle, what don't you have on?" Gail and Sabrina high five each other and laughed. "This bitch is damn near naked" was what Sabrina said to Gail.

Michelle laughed and sat down at the table, while looking out the corner of her eye to see if Josh was looking at her, And just as she suspected he was. He was watching her every chance he could.

Michelle knew that Josh was watching too, that was why when Gail and Sabrina said what they did; she did not make a big deal of it. She felt that they help her to get the attention from Josh that she was seeking.

It was time to put the meat on the grill, Gary walked over to the table to get the meat that was going on the grill first.

When he did of course Gail was still sitting there with Sabrina, this was the first time Gary was nervous to come around Sabrina and Gail together.

Only because he did not know how to hide what he was really feeling, Gail being the naive person that she is never suspected anything. Sabrina, hell did not care one way or another. David and Josh were still talking at the grill, at this time they were drinking their beers and laughing as men do. Josh in his mind had to figure out a way to get Michelle alone so he could find out was she what he was really after. Josh figured that a woman that he was after would do what he wanted and went he wanted.

That is pretty much how he would describe his type of woman, looks were not important to Josh because he had one plan in mind. For her to give him head, as he would say it "hell, I don't have to look at her"

Although Josh could stand and talk with the fellows, he caught himself watching Michelle. Gail naïve to the street life had a certain intuition about her. If she suspected something ninety percent of the time, she was right.

Gail knew Josh just wanted Michelle for one thing "what she could do for him" But how do she tell Michelle? Without making Michelle feel that she was "just in her business" as Michelle would say it.

Michelle and Gail did not have the sister relationship that they should have. Sabrina and Gail had a relationship that was more like a sister-to-sister relationship then they did.

Gail wondered if it was simply sibling rivalry. Alternatively, did their age play a major factor?

Michelle always acted as if she was the older sister

because she had the street wisdom. This would cause a conflict between the two of them at times; Michelle just did not want to listen to nothing Gail told her. Michelle would purposely do the opposite.

After everyone ate, Gary wanted to know if they all wanted to come by the house to play cards and pick up where the barbeque left off. Michelle said "I'll be by later I have to run a errand before I come"

Josh, Sabrina and David agreed to come by but wanted to go home to freshen up. Therefore, everyone pack up their belonging and head towards their cars. Josh walks Michelle to her car and ask if she is coming for sure, because if she was not he would call it a day.

He said he did not want to be the only one at the house without a date. Michelle turns and asks so you are asking? Josh replied, "I guess I am" Gary's main idea of inviting everyone is so he could somehow get to talk to Sabrina about possibly getting together.

David and Sabrina on the way home in their car talk and David tell her that he was sorry for ever thinking that his friend Gary wanted her. Sabrina knowing what she said to Gary just tell David not to worry about it

Sabrina thinking to herself "hell Gary just don't want me, I want him as well" However, Sabrina wanted Gary just for what she could get out of him; on the other hand, Gary wanted Sabrina for her body.

Before going to Gary and Gail's, David wanted Sabrina to call to see what they wanted to drink because he was stopping at the store.

Sabrina called and Gary answered the phone. Sabrina asked what they were drinking. And Gary said " I wish it could be you" Sabrina replied ok I'll get you all something because David was standing close and she couldn't make it obvious that what Gary just said.

At Gail and Gary's house everyone started coming, Davis and Sabrina got there first. Gail invited them into the dining room where they would play cards. Sabrina sat down at the table David gave Gary the bags.

David sits down at the table and asks, "So what's it going to be? Spades or Bid Whist?" They laugh at him and Gail say "you know it's Spades" that way when Michelle and Josh get here we can play a process of elimination.

The game begins and Michelle and Josh arrive close to the same time. The first hand Gail and Gary won, then as the game go on, the two of them were eliminated. Someone make a suggestion of splitting the teams up, Now David is on Gail's team.

As the game continued Gary went into the kitchen to get more ice for the bucket. Sabrina found a way to need to go into the kitchen. She said "Let me see what is taking Mr. slow poke so long with the ice"

The card game is so intensified until no one noticed what she said. Sabrina walks into the kitchen and Gary turn as she entered the room. She asks him "what's taking so long?" Gary said, "You got me so hot until the ice kept melting" Sabrina laughs.

They both know that they cannot be to long because Gail or David might come. Gary grabs Sabrina and kisses her while he squeezes her ass.

"Damn, this was better than I imagined" Gary said as he let her go. He tells her "I want you to take my cell number and call me so we can get away, ok?" He writes the number down on a piece of paper bag and Sabrina put it quickly in her bra. Sabrina had to be the first out of the kitchen so no one think anything happened.

As she goes back into the dining room, she has to say something to make it seem like Gary is coming now with the ice. She says "Here he comes with his slow butt, he act like he was freezing it" They laugh at her and this helped with her plan to keep the attention off them.

Gary enters the room with the bucket of ice; he sat it down on the table. Josh and Michelle were eliminated from the game and walked outside. While outside Josh kissed Michelle, during the kissing Josh run his hand underneath her skirt.

She did not have panties on, Josh got very excited about this. His penis hardened, he wanted her now and his kissing intensified her curiosity to know how he made love. She whispered in his ear "how about getting a room and we can finish this there" Josh was more than happy to oblige.

Josh was so happy about him was getting Michelle to go to a room until he told her "You go tell everyone good night for me and I will go ahead and get the room" Josh leave.

Michelle goes back inside and tells everyone that she was leaving, when asked where Josh was? She say "oh yeah he told me to tell you all he was leaving and would see you all later"

Gail say "He didn't even say goodnight" Gary and David laugh and say " That man is on a mission" the two of them knew what Josh had told them earlier about getting into Michelle's panties.

David and Sabrina go home after their visit because it's late into the night but Sabrina go to bed thinking about tomorrow and how she could call Gary. Gail never suspected anything was going on and she and Gary go to bed as well.

# Sexual Betrayal

Gail woke up and Gary was already gone, she thought to herself "damn, I must have over slept" She look over at the clock, its seven thirty. It was her usual time that she woke up.

Gail thought "Gary must have left for work earlier than he usually did" because she did not hear him leave. Gary was anticipating Sabrina's call. He was thinking if he got to work early if she called him then he could leave early.

Gary cell phone begun to ring, he had to find where it was. He could hear it, but it was in his pocket. He found it before it stopped. Gary looked at the screen to make sure it was Sabrina calling.

He figured it was her, since the call was from a number that he did not recognize. He answered in an "I have been waiting for your call voice" but he did not want Sabrina to think that he was desperate.

"Hello" was Gary's response. The voice on the other end just stated "The pussy's yours if you come get it now" then come a voice of Sabrina laughing. Gary said "Sabrina" she said "who else is it, silly ass man" Gary did not know how to response to this because to him pussy never was thrown at his so easily.

He did not think about anything but how to get it and when he could. He asked her "so where are you?" Sabrina said "I'm downtown in a room laying butt naked with my legs apart waiting on that dick" Gary said "Look if you want me to get it, you have to be more specific than that"

No on the real "I'm downtown at the Jefferson Hotel, the room number is 123" and Gary, you have to pay me back for the room. I am not paying for the room for you to fuck me. Gary told her that he would pay her back and said he would be there.

Before Gary could leave the job his phone rung again, this time he didn't look at the screen he just answered it and replied " I said I was on my way" the voice on the phone said "on your was where?" it was Gail. "Oh, hey baby" Gary's nervously responded, I thought you was Josh. I just hung up from him and told him that I would pick him up from work because his car broke down. Gail said "well don't he have road service?"

Gary said I did not ask him, he asked if I could come get him and told him I would. Gail said "ok" but how long will you be? Gary said as soon as I am done I will be home. Gary knew he had to call Josh now so that Josh did not call their house looking for him.

If Josh called, where would Gary tell Gail he was at or what if Gail questioned Josh? Gary got on the phone desperately calling Josh "hello this is Josh, I'm unable to take your call leave a message at the beep" Damn it, where is Josh? Was all Gary thought. He had to talk to Josh before Gail did or he would be busted.

In addition he kept in mind that Sabrina was waiting on him, how long would she wait before she would be calling back asking what was taking so long? Gary decided that he would continue to go meet Sabrina while trying to call Josh.

Driving downtown its lunchtime and the traffic is back up. The lodge freeway is under construction so Gary had to drive down Woodward, the long route.

Time is going by so fast; at least Gary thought it was. How much time will this allow him to be with Sabrina since Gail was waiting at home on him? Gary try calling Josh again, Josh phone ring, "hello" Josh answers. Gary talking with slight relief "man, I'm glad to hear your voice" Josh somewhat surprised "what's up?" Gary tells Josh "I need you to cover for me"

Josh laugh, "who is she?" Gary said "Josh come on man you know better" Josh said "Gary now man you know I know you and if you need me to cover for you, you got something up" Gary said just listen; I told Gail that I was picking you from work because your car broke down. So do not call the house I will call you when I am finished. Josh said "Ok, but you have to tell me who she is.

They hang up the phone, now Gary feel like its going to work out. He is on his way to meet Sabrina and Gail thinks he is with Josh. Gary get to the hotel, he park his car and look for room 123. He walk looking at each door as he approached the door, Sabrina opens it. Come on in I have been waiting. As he walk in she was standing slightly behind it because she was completely naked.

She closed the door behind Gary and jump on him knocking him to the bed. While lying on him naked, she asks, "so let me see if what Gail told me about you is true" in this case the anticipation was better than the wait.

Gary unzipped his pants and pulled out what Sabrina was highly pissed about. His penis was as big as that of a male child. Sabrina thought to herself "he better know how to eat pussy because his dick was too little to do anything for her"

She know she could not stop here she had to go all the way, so she played the role. After Gary was finish Sabrina still not satisfied he knew, so he begun licking her all over. He got between her thighs and then he got straight to where she wanted him.

Well at least he could eat pussy well enough for her to climax and she did. Gary lying half-asleep, Sabrina got up and said "Gary it's time to go" Gary stagger to the bathroom to wash up while Sabrina said "hey, don't forget you own me for this room"

Gary asked how much? Sabrina said thirty-five dollars. He walked to where his pants fell on the floor and went into his pocket. He pulled out his wallet and gave her the money, He was the first to leave but she left not far behind. They did not want to be seen leaving together.

However, before leaving Gary asked "Can we do this again?" Sabrina told him she would call him. Gary knew that meant "no" but at least out right she did not say it like that.

Gary got in his car and drove home, Gail wanted him to make love to her but he was too tired from Sabrina. Sabrina was mad as hell, she betrayed her friend for something that was not worth the wait for.

Gail called Sabrina while she was driving home and she did not answer he phone. Sabrina's guilt was too much for her to talk to Gail right now.

The next day Gail called Sabrina and she still did not answer, she then called her house out of concern if she was all right. David answered and said Sabrina was ok but she was not at home.

A couple of days passed and Gail noticed she was having a smelly discharge. She made a doctors appointment. When she got to the doctor's office she walked to the receptionist desk and the receptionist was on the phone.

The receptionist was telling someone on the phone about how this nasty ass girl that comes into the office had gave a man a STD and he is married. Now she has to tell the man and she knows he will freak out on her.

Gail in her mind was thinking about how nasty that girl was to have a STD and on top of it she was fucking someone else's husband. She said to herself "poor wife, I wouldn't want to be in her shoes" To find out this way that your husband was cheating oh boy, There would be hell to tell.

The receptionist call Gail to take her into an exam room. "The doctor will be right with you" Mrs. Halsey is what the receptionist said. After waiting for about ten minutes he door opened to where Gail was waiting, in came a doctor with his nurse as his assistant.

He told her that she had to take off her pants and drape herself with a piece of paper he handed her. He and the nurse then begin the exam; the doctor took some cultures and told Gail he would give her an antibiotic because she definitely had a discharge.

He also told her when the tests come back from the cultures his office would call her if she needed to come back. Gary was having problems too, so he wanted to talk to Sabrina and ask her if she was.

He called her and she did not answer her phone. On his lunch break Gary went to the social clinic, to see if he had something.

He told Josh about how his penis was leaking a fluid

and Josh told him "man, whoever you been with gave you Chlamydia" all Gary thought about was if he gave it to Gail? Gary knew Sabrina was the only person besides Gail he had sex with.

When Gary got to the clinic it was confirmed Sabrina had gave him a STD, now how could he find out if Gail got it. How would he explain this if she did? Gail was not sure what was going on with her so she did not want to tell Gary because if it was something serious she wanted to ask Sabrina what she thought about it.

The only problem was Sabrina was not returning her calls. Gail telephone rung back to her and she thought it was Sabrina calling her but it was the doctor's office. "Mrs. Halsey?" was what the voice said. "Yes, this is she" was Gail's response.

This is Dr. Alexander's office calling and you need to come back into the office, how about tomorrow at noon? Is everything ok? Is what Gail wanted to know. The receptionist told her that the doctor wanted to talk to her. This worried Gail because what could be wrong that the doctor wanted her back at his office.

Too Much Trust

When Gary came home Gail did not tell him what was going on, she wanted to wait until she got back from the doctor office. Gary told Gail that his job needed him to go out of town for training, they were getting new machines and everyone had to do training for it.

Gail wanted to know how long the training was. He told her it was only for a couple of weeks but the time would go fast. Gail as always was so trusting of Gary until she agreed and still did not mention what was going on with her.

Meanwhile she continued to try to call Sabrina. She wanted to tell her and maybe she could help her understand the discharge. Gail waited until Gary was not in the room and picked up the phone to call Sabrina.

Sabrina phone rang and David answered "Hello" Hi David this is Gail and I have been trying to get in touch with Sabrina, is she there? "Yes" just one minute was what David said.

"Hello" this time Sabrina came to the phone. "Hey girl" where you been? I have called you many times and could not get you. "yeah I know" but I' been running around and by the time I get finish it's late and I could get back to you, was the explanation Sabrina had.

Gail did not focus on the answer, she was just glad Sabrina was on the phone. Gail goes on to tell Sabrina about the problem that she has, and ask her do she know what it could be.

Sabrina pauses "Oh girl you know I been hearing that it's been going around with the other girls"

Gail asks is it bad? Sabrina knowing that she was lying

said "no, girl it's just a discharge and you should go to the doctor he will give you something for it"

Sabrina knew what it was because she had it too, she gave Gary Chlamydia and he gave it to Gail. She had to some how sneak and give David his medicine in his food so he did not know that she had it. Therefore, when she cooked dinner she crushed the pills up in David food and he never knew he took it.

While eating the food David said "Sabrina why you put so much salt in the spaghetti?" Little did he know that Sabrina was trying to drown out the pill taste. On the other hand, Sabrina had a plan for Gary too; she had to somehow get Gary to go out with her again. Moreover, she knew he would be anxious to go to a room but this time she was not going.

After talking to Gail, Sabrina planned how she could get Gary to take the pills. She thought to herself "I'll get him to drank it in his in a soda" Sabrina had it all figured out. Sabrina knew she had to go with Gail to the doctor office so that she could make sure Gail did not find out what really was going on.

Sabrina called Gail back and suggested that she go along to the doctor's office as support. Gail insisted that she would ok but Sabrina convinced her that she could tell her everything that the doctor was saying so Gail could understand.

Sabrina did it again, she out smarted Gail into letting her go. At the doctors office Sabrina knew the receptionist and told her to make sure that they do not tell Gail what was going on.

She told them that Gail had a nervous breakdown before and could not handle this sort of news, that was why she came along.

The receptionist did not question Sabrina; she agreed that this would be the right way to handle it. However, she did say it was not her call it was totally up to the doctor whether or not he told Gail.

The receptionist was hesitant about asking the doctor to do this but she did and to her surprise he agreed. He did not want to cause a disturbance in the office because there were too many patients waiting to be seen.

After the receptionist told the doctor, he thought it would be better to hurry and get Gail seen so she could leave the office quickly. He felt the quicker she was seen the less likely she could cause a disturbance.

Sabrina waited patiently to see if the doctor did agree because the receptionist did not tell her if he would right away. When the receptionist call Sabrina back to the desk she just knew that it would be to tell her that the doctor did not agreed to this, but she was wrong.

All odds were in Sabrina favor, now to get Gail treatment so she could take her back home because she still had to get Gary cured too. Sabrina was so out cold with her ways until she decided to call Gay while she was with Gail.

She knew she could not call his name out because Gail was in the next seat from her. Sabrina was getting a kick out of all of this, to call a man and be sitting next to his wife.

This gave her an adrenalin rush, and made her feel like she was indeed all that. She dialed the number and the phone begun to ring, after about the third ring Gary answers "Hello" Sabrina start talking without saying his name " You know I thought about what you asked and I think I'm up to it"

Gary knew her voice and was excited, he thought she meant she would go to another room with him, but she did not. Therefore, he asked "the same hotel?" Sabrina quickly said, "I just want us to go hang out for a bit, maybe get a drink or two"

Gary did not think this was a good idea because he said, "what if someone sees us together?" Sabrina told him that she had it all figured out where and what they were going to do. He asked her did she have a time in mind. She replied I am busy right now, but I will get back to you on the time and place.

Gail could hear the conversation from Sabrina but had no idea Gary was who she was talking to. They hung up and Gail teased her "you cheating on David? Sabrina said no that was a close friend and I am going to meet him for a drink after I drop you off at home.

Gail did not let it go she then said, "Was it someone we went to school with?" Sabrina said no and stop with the interrogations.Gail continued on to say now I see why you couldn't get back to me whenever I called you, you were busy with Mr. secret identity.

Sabrina laughed at her but managed to get her attention away from this conversation fast. Gail was like a puppet when it came down to Sabrina; Sabrina was pulling her by her strings. Sabrina took Gail home and decided now would be the best time to call Gary back. Sabrina dialed Gary cell phone back he answers " Hello" Sabrina in her trying to be sexy voice ask "so can we meet now?"

Gary told her that he was leaving his job and asks where she has in mind. Her response was "we can meet downtown then go over to Canada, this way no one could possibly see us"

Gary thought this way a very good idea but he also had in mind maybe he could get her to go a room. Sabrina had one thing on her mind, to get him to take the medicine.

They hang up the phone and she knew she had to call David. She call home but David was not there. She then called his cell phone; it goes straight to his voice mail. "Where could he be?" was what Sabrina thought. However she did not care much about finding out, she wanted to hurry and meet Gary so she could go home.

Traffic is heavy as usual going downtown this time of the day. The Lodge freeway is still closed and she too had to drive down Woodward. The closer she got downtown the thicker the traffic got.

She thought about "maybe I'll get off Woodward and take another way" The direction that she was traveling she seen the ambassador bridge, so she knew she was downtown.

When she stopped, she called to see where Gary was.
He told her that he was maybe ten minutes from her and
he would be there shortly.

Sabrina sat in her car and listened to the radio. It was
getting dark outside and she wanted Gary to hurry up so
that if David came home and she was not there, he
would not call looking for her.

She was sitting in a parking lot and every time and car pulled in she look in her rear view mirror to see if it was Gary. Soon Gary did come; he parked his car beside hers and got into Sabrina car.

They headed across the bridge to Canada. He look over at her and asked her "well, are you glad to see me?" Sabrina in her cunning way said "more than you know" Gary had no idea what he was in store for.

Gary continued talking and asked her "so why didn't you give me a hug or kiss" Sabrina told Gary "look buddy we didn't just meet ok" you and I are just fucking partners. It is not going to be as if I give you kisses and hugs when we see each other.

Gary was too embarrassed to respond, he thought Sabrina really wanted him. Now he was having second thoughts on it. However to himself he thought "Why was she sneaking with him?"

Gary never asked her, he just was glad he has the opportunity to get extra ass when he want it, so he thought. Sabrina had in mind Gary was extra money to her. Hell, if that meant fucking him from time to time then that is what she would do.

Sabrina drove until she got to this Chinese restaurant, parked the car and told Gary "ok, this is where I want to go" Gary not believing his eyes said "You wanted to eat?" Sabrina said no "I told you I wanted to go for drinks"

Gary said but I thought we would get a room and….Sabrina cut him off before he could finish his statement. "Gary, if you want this pussy at leisure then you is going to have to pay to play"

The first fuck was on the house but now the courtesy is over, how much money you got? Damn girl you do not waste no time do you. Was Gary's reply. Sabrina said hell no, if I just want some dick I got David.

The fuck was a courtesy to you, now you have to pay for the good shit she said patting herself. Gary laughed and said "Well I can't argue with you on that, it was good" Sabrina pulled her panties down, rubbed her vagina and asked Gary if he wanted to smell it?

Gary said "why are you teasing me, are you going to let me have some if I do?" Sabrina pulled her panties back up and said lets go eat. When they got out of the car, they could see back across to the United States side of the border.

Sabrina had to say something smart, she said, "across there somewhere is David and Gail and they would never imagine we are here" then she begin to laugh. They walk inside the restaurant and sat down at a table.

The waiter came over and handed them menus, he ask what do they want to drink? Sabrina said "for me coke and you Gary?" As she look at him. Gary say "That's fine I'll have a coke also" The waiter tell them he would return for their order.

A minute or so go by and the waiter return giving them their cokes. "Are you ready to order?" was his next question. Sabrina knew what she wanted but Gary took a little more time and then said "I'll have the number two combination"

The waiter took the menus as he leave the table, Gary tell Sabrina he has to go to the bathroom and he would be right back. Perfect is what Sabrina thought, now this is her time to give him the medicine in his coke.

Sabrina told Gary "take your time because the food is not ready anyway" Gary could not get in the bathroom fast enough; Sabrina had the pills out and opened. She shook the powder into Gary's glass and stirred it up with her spoon.

Gary returned right after the ice stop moving in the glass from the stirring. He sat down and made a comment "Now I can start over" as he picked up his glass and drank the coke.

Sabrina watched Gary drank the coke as if she was waiting to see what he thought about it. Gary did not mention that the coke tasted different so Sabrina was at ease. The waiter came to the table with the food and they ate.

Gary said "Sabrina are we going home after or to a room?" Sabrina said that really depends on you, I asked do you have any money. You never told me if you did or not. Gary being egotistical respond "I always have money"

This was something Sabrina knew, that is why she was with him for the money he made. Sabrina insisted that they just go home for now, but they would get together another time to go to a room.

Once again, she told Gary that she would call him when she could get with him again. After leaving the restaurant Gary and Sabrina drove back across the ambassador bridge and back into reality of their every day lives.

Gary slid One hundred and fifty dollars to Sabrina and said "Thanks for meeting with me" Gary got out of Sabrina car and into his car.

By his demeanor Sabrina could tell his disappointment he most likely wanted to get a room while they were together, but after the first experience that was something Sabrina was trying to avoid.

Sabrina thought to herself "what easy money" He is a real sucker and I am going to like getting the extra money.

As Sabrina thought about his penis size, she knew he and Gail were married before they had sex or else she probably would have called it off. Then again the way Gail talk to Sabrina about how good Gary is in bed, she might enjoy his size.

Something's money cannot buy and to marry him with his little penis is one of them. The drive home was faster than Sabrina thought it would be, maybe because Sabrina was thinking about Gary's size and laughing to herself.

Sometime when Gail start to talk about how good Gary is to her is in bed, Sabrina wanted to tell her "stop lying; his penis is so damn small" However, if she did Gail would know Sabrina saw it and how could she explain that?

David is what Sabrina and the other dancers call "a man with blessings" If the other dancers and Sabrina thought a man had a large penis they would make sure they said "Have a blessed night" before he leave the club.

The dancers and Sabrina laughed because we knew what "have a blessed night meant" refering to his penis, the man would not know though he would think that was their way of saying take care.

As she approach her house, Sabrina could can see that David car was not in the driveway, so he was not home yet. It was going on eight o' clock and she showered then watched television. An hour later David came in the door.

"Hey baby" was his response. "Hello dear" is what she said back to him. So how was your day? He asked next. She told him that it was long and very tiresome, but she was glad it is over.

David asks "Did you eat?" while he look into the refrigerator. "I had a little something before coming home" was what she said but Sabrina was thinking about the big ass Chinese meal that she just had with Gary.

In addition, how she got his ass to take those pills were her thoughts. David said "Well I guess that I will go back out to get myself something to eat because I haven't eaten anything since lunch"

I was going to stop and get something but thought I would come home first to make sure that you had eaten. Sabrina asks "Why you didn't call, David?" David response was 'I did, you didn't answer' Oh; I had to be in the shower Sabrina said.

Sabrina knew that she just got home herself. David put his coat back on and heads for the door, as he opens it he turns and asks Sabrina if she want anything? Sabrina looks up towards the ceiling as if she was trying to think of something that she might want.

"Nah" I am good but thanks for asking, Sabrina answers as she turns the television channel. The telephone rung as David shut the door; he was not quite off the porch so he could tell it was Gail calling by what he heard Sabrina saying. "Hey girl, whats going on?" Sabrina said loud enough for David to hear from the porch as he was leaving. Gail was on the phone telling Sabrina for some strange reason she is beginning not to trust Gary. Sabrina wants to know why Gail felt that way. "Because lately he wasn't as attentive as he normally was" Gail told Sabrina. Gail goes on to tell Sabrina how he was starting to come home later and later.

Sabrina being defensive, tell Gail "ah girl he is probably working later" that is all. Sabrina tells Gail that she is worrying for nothing and that she know how Gary felt about her.

Yeah but Sabrina also knew how Gary felt about her too. Sabrina was just playing the role as friend to Gail like the one she always did. Gail so trusting of Sabrina listened "yes you're right, Gary loves me and he wouldn't jeopedize our marriage for no sleezy woman in the street"

Sabrina laughing inside because she knew that she was the sleezy woman that Gail was refering too. Gail felt at ease after talking to Sabrina but little did Gail know Sabrina was the woman seeing Gary behind her back and now Sabrina has a plan on how she is going to get Gary's money without all the sex.

As Gail and Sabrina continued to talk Gail asks Sabrina so what did you do today? Sabrina is so used to having a quick come back lie until it did not take her long to think of the answer.

"Girl, I really didn't do much" Sabrina said quickly. Gail then asks, "Well did you go downtown? "Um, Um no" why you ask? Sabrina wanted to know, so she could make sure that she and Gary were not seen together before going to Canada. Sabrina thought how strange it was for Gail to ask about her going downtown when that is where she and Gary met. Talk about coincidence, Sabrina was wondering if Gary dumb ass got so mad that she did not have sex with him until he went home and confessed it all. Sabrina was thinking if that were the case, what her explanation would be to

David. Sabrina thought about how she was not to much worried about Gail, hell if Gail ask me why I did it I will kick her ass.

Sabrina snaps out of the thought when Gail continued to say "Sabrina, Sabrina did you hear me girl?" Sabrina appologize and say "no girl my mind was somewhere else sorry what did you just say?"

Gail laughed "Sabrina that must have been a crazy thought because I was asking you if you went downtown to meet with your friend for a drink?" Sabrina you said you would meet with him "well did you?" Gail said in between her laughing.

Sabrina responded, oh girl I did not get to go because I was just working around the house and the time got by me. Sabrina did say that she was going tomorrow and she would call her after she gets back. Yes because I want to know what you did and you have to tell me everything, Gail said like Sabrina was cheating on David and she wanted to know all the details about the affair.

Sabrina said there is not going to be much to tell I am just meeting him for a drink not giving him head and they both laugh. Sabrina tell Gail "well, girl I'll call you later David is coming and I want to see what he want to eat for dinner"

Gail said oh, ok talk with you later. Sabrina constantly laughed at Gail for being so damn stupid, Sabrina knew that David was not coming.

David just walked out the door before she answered the phone but that was Sabrina's way of getting Gail off the phone.

David was driving to the restaurant but he had his own agenda too before picking up his food, he was going to have some fun in Cass corridor. Cass corridor, everyone knew that if you were looking for a prostitute this is the area to go.

Sabrina got dressed and went to the club early so she could work.

# Night Stroll

The hidden past of David was coming out at night when Sabrina was at the club working. David liked the company he kept with the local prostitutes in Cass Corridor.

He drove down Third Street a little while until he pulled up to two girls that flashed their ass to him as he approached them.

"What's happening mama?" is what David asked as the two girl's leaned onto the door of his car. One of the girls was leaning so hard her breasts were practically out of her shirt.

David did not mind this at all because he was getting a free look at what he thought he could have his mouth on later. What you looking for baby? Was what the other girl asked. David said what you got.

The girl looked at him then said "You are not a fucking cop are you? David replied "no baby why would you ask that?" the girl look at him and said because baby you are in the corridor and there is one of two things you could want.

That is ass or drugs. So what you want? Usually when the people come here, they just flat out ask for what they want, they do not ask us what we got. Hell they know. I am not trying to sell no drugs with all this money getter I got, pointing to her ass.

David was no virgin to the streets in the corridor either; he knew what was going on. That was just his way to see if the girls were working undercover or if they were really what he was looking for, a prostitute. David asks, "So do I get to have both of you?" The girl with her breast hanging partially out responds "If your money is right you can have whatever you want"

This sound good to me is what David said. David telephone rung "Hello" David answers. It is Sabrina calling she asks "so what you doing?" David could not tell her he was in Cass corridor trying to buy ass, so he made up a story how he wanted to go buy some beer from the store.

Sabrina asks "Don't we have beer in the refrigerator? David with his smart rebuttal tells her "now if we had beer, why do you think I would be going to the store?"

Just as Sabrina could come up with a rebuttal to someone, David was the same way he could too. Sabrina then told David that the club is slow and she would be home early. David was glad she called, so this would tell him how much time he had to do his dirt.

The girls at his car knew to be quiet because as David phone begin to ring David put his fingers up to his mouth and motioned for them to be. When Sabrina hung the phone up, the girls continued to negotiate their prices to David.

David knew he did not have much more time so he pretended that the price was too much. This made the girls angry and turn away from his car while cursing at him and yelling out "Man, the price isn't high your fucking bitch just called and you got to run like a whore"

David could not let the girls have the last word before he pulled off; he had to get his words in too. David drove pass them and said, "You two look like hell is why I didn't want your funky shit anyway"

Now David knew he had to go buy beer so Sabrina did not know he was lying if she got home and did not see any extra beer. David knew that there was beer at home so he just brought a couple of can's to go along with what he had already.

David drove back home from the store just in time before Sabrina got home. He could not have been at home no more then twenty minutes, when he heard Sabrina car pull into the driveway.

David met her at the door, "so how was your night?" He asks as he takes her bag from her. Sabrina tell David how the club was slow so the manager asks who wanted to leave and since she didn't feel much like working, she decided she would.

David tells Sabrina that this is ok; now the two of them could watch a movie and drink beer or something. Sabrina was cool with this so that is what they did before going to bed. When morning came, Sabrina called Gail to see if she wanted to start exercising with her and Sabrina's mother.

Sabrina suggested that they join Sabrina's mother walking in the park. Sabrina and Gail both agree that they both could afford to lose some weight.

Sabrina mother walk everyday in the park in the afternoon, Sabrina tell Gail that she would pick her up at four o'clock and to be ready and that Sabrina mother would meet them at the park.

Just as she said Sabrina was at Gail's house blowing her horn in the driveway at four o'clock yelling "Gail come on girl we have to go" Gail ran out the door allowing the screen to slam behind her.

Sabrina was sitting in her car with the music so loud until if Gail did tell her she would be right there she would not have heard her. As Gail got into the car, Sabrina reaches over and turns the radio down.

She ask Gail "so are you ready to walk that fat away?" laughing. Gail look at her and ask "Why do you always have to have a smart ass mouth?" Gail laugh. Sabrina look up at the car ceiling and she say "Um, because I'm a smart ass chick" Gail tell Sabrina "you got that right, you are definitely a smart ass chick alright" but Gail response was meant to be sarcastic.

Sabrina drove toward the park as she approached she begin to look for her mother. There were so may people until they could not see her if she was right in front of them.

Sabrina mother saw them so she begins to wave her arms in the air, so they could see her. Sabrina parks the car and she and Gail got out then started to walk towards Sabrina mother. As they got closer Sabrina asks her mother "Mama, you remember Gail?" Sabrina mother said "Sure I do"

Sabrina mother told them "come on girls lets get started" as she begin to stretch her legs out. After they stretched out, they begun to walk around the park. As they walked around Sabrina see and old class mate, Robert.

 Robert if you look at him you knew he was was sick or a crack head, he was so skinny and his hygiene was very poor. Robert approached Sabrina with the look of surprise on his face. The two of them embraced, Sabrina say "man how you been?" It has been a long time since I have seen you, Sabrina turn and introduce

Robert to Gail and her mother. Sabrina mother smiled, Robert and Sabrina exchange telephone numbers and say their goodbyes.

Robert walked across the street, Sabrina mother ask Sabrina about Robert. Sabrina tells her "he was a classmate from years ago"

As they walk away, they turned to see this white cargo van pull up beside Robert, three men got out of the van. One of the men who's name is Scott walk in front of the other two men. Scott was known in the neighborhood as a major drug seller.

All the men walk toward Robert, from across the street they could see that Scott grabbing then pinned Robert against the building. Scott had his hands gripping tightly around Robert's collar.

They could not hear what was being said, but knew Scott was obviously angry. There was screaming of words towards Robert. The other men stood watching as if they were waiting for Robert to run or fight back.

A crowd of people from the park stood watching, they knew they do not want to be involved so they continued to walk away. Sabrina and Gail have a conversation about what possibly could be happening.

Sabrina suggested that Robert probably owed Scott money for drugs. Gail never offered her opinion she just listened to Sabrina and wondered if Sabrina was correct with what she said.

Gail and Sabrina continued to walk talking when Sabrina noticed that her mother was not with them. Sabrina asks "Where is my mother?" Gail respond "I don't know? I didn't notice that she wasn't with us" Since there were so many people standing around watching the commotion from Scott neither of the girls noticed when Sabrina mother left.

Sabrina was now in a panic, where could her mother be. Sabrina told Gail "we need to go back and see if we can find my mother"

The two of them returned to the area where the entire ruckus was but they did not see Sabrina's mother. This worried Sabrina, she asks Gail if she had a cellular telephone.

Gail told Sabrina that her telephone was at home, she left it in a rush to leave when Sabrina was blowing her horn in the driveway.

They noticed the van pulling away, the van sped pass and the sound coming from the van, told them that Robert was inside but was Sabrina's mother with him. Why the men took, Robert was a question in their mind.

Sabrina and Gail got into Sabrina car so that they could find a pay phone. Sabrina first thought was maybe her mother did not see them so she went home. They found a pay phone and Sabrina got out of the car.

Sabrina pick up the telephone receiver "damn the phone don't work" Sabrina said as she hung the receiver up slamming it. Sabrina walk back to the car and got in, cursing she asked Gail "why don't any of these fucking telephone's work on the street?"

Gail wanted to respond but did not because she knew Sabrina was angry. Sabrina finally found a working phone and called her mothers house but there was not an answer. Sabrina wondered where her mother could be.

Driving though the neighborhood, Gail and Sabrina ask questions about Robert. Maybe Robert could tell them where Sabrina mother was. Some of the people they spoke with told them that they did not want to be involved only because Robert owed a drug debt.

This could be the reason they saw Robert get practically beating up at the park. There was not a question in their mind about who Robert owed the money either.

Nevertheless, why did Sabrina mother just disappear? Could she be with Robert and if so, why?

Gail thought Sabrina was concerned but not hysterically concerned as she would have been if it had been her mother.

Gail knew Sabrina was ghetto but it was not to the point where Sabrina would mess with Scott. Sabrina and Gail ran across these people sitting on the stairs of an abandon house, the people told them they could find Scott at the flame bar.

Sabrina told Gail "we can't just walk into the bar Scott know me" If Scott saw her then he would know why she was there. Gail told Sabrina if her mother was missing then she would not care if Scott did see her, he would have to tell me what the fuck was going on.

The flame bar was Scott's hang out, so all his thug friends more than likely would be around. Scott never traveled alone, so he probably was not as hard as he acted.

Why the other people followed him, I wondered. It was probably because Scott had money. I bet any of the people if giving the chance would knock him off if they could.

Gail told Sabrina "you know I would do as much as I could for you, but this one you need to let the police handle" I rather go home. Sabrina asked Gail "what you scared?" I thought you were my girl.

Gail reply "I am but Scott is ruthless and would beat his mother if money was involved" Sabrina angrily say "Scott isn't shit!"

Yeah Sabrina said that to me but she would not have the same attitude if Scott were here in front of us. Gail insisted she wanted to go home and Sabrina could call her later. Sabrina said "ok chicken shit I'll take you home" She was glad Sabrina finally agreed with her, she never was this glad to be at home before in her life. After experiencing this, Gail would not drive with Sabrina again.

If Sabrina wants to meet somewhere, Gail would drive herself. This taught her not only was Sabrina trouble but her mother was as well.

Sabrina drove herself to the flame bar and thought that she could confront Scott about her mother; Sabrina could give a damn about Robert.

Sabrina Park her car, the parking lot is full so she knew she would have to find Scott once she got inside the bar. Scott would see her before she saw him if he was watching the door when Sabrina walked in.

Sabrina approached the bar door, people were going inside. The door attendant is searching everyone one at a time. Sabrina stood to the side letting people in front of her.

A person named Bruce walk by, he notices Sabrina. Bruce ask "hey girl what you doing here?" Sabrina told Bruce "I just came to see what the competition was doing" they both laugh.

Bruce asks "Are you alone?" Sabrina hesitated but answers "yes" Sabrina did not want to make it obvious that she was looking for Scott.

Scott has many loyal followers so how could Sabrina know that Bruce is not one of them.

Bruce asks Sabrina since you are alone you should join me for a drink.

Sabrina figure walking in with Bruce would help her because if someone she knew saw her, it would not be so obvious that she was really looking for Scott.

Sabrina walk ahead of Bruce through the door, the crowd inside was loud. Sabrina looks around through the crowd as she walks in, hoping to spot Scott somewhere. The bar was so dark until unless you were close to the person you were talking too you really could not see them

The people sitting at the bar were more prominent, mainly because they were in more light. Sabrina told Bruce that she wanted to sit in a booth only because this would allow her to see around the room better.

Bruce did not mind where they sat, Knowing Bruce he would not be doing much sitting anyway. All it took was for Bruce to see one of his homey's and Sabrina would be sitting by alone in the booth.

 The server came to the table and asks if they were ready to order. Sabrina order a screwdriver on the rocks and Bruce order a beer.

The server tells them she would be right back with their order. Bruce pull out twenty dollars and tell Sabrina to pay for the drinks, he had to use the men's room.

The server came back to the table after a few minutes; she came back with the order before Bruce came out the men's room.

Sabrina paid for the drinks and the server left. Sabrina looks at her watch and notice that Bruce was gone for at least ten minutes

Sabrina was wondering what was taking Bruce so long in the men's room. Sabrina drink was nearly gone and Bruce still wasn't back, the waitress came back to the table this time she told Sabrina "that young man you were with paid me to tell you he left"

"Left? What do you mean left? The server said he told me to wait about ten minutes then tell you he was gone. Sabrina wondered why Bruce would leave like that. Hell, they were not on a date. She came to the bar alone anyway. While looking around and wondering about Bruce, Sabrina did not notice Scott coming from the other direction.

Scott noticed her, he slid into the booth so smooth until he scared Sabrina when she looked up and he was sitting there. "So, Miss Sabrina what bring you here?" Scott questioned.

Sabrina did not want Scott to notice her nervousness, she responded "just to see what the other side of town was doing"

Scott asks "are you sure you were checking me out?" Sabrina quickly replied "Checking you out, for what?" Scott told Sabrina come on girl I am from the street as well as you are.

Scott continues to say why after the little ride I gave Robert and your mammy you decide to check out the flame.

Well speaking of my mother, where is she? Scott pointing his finger at Sabrina replies "I knew it was you I saw at the park earlier" Yes, it was me you saw but where is my mother? Sabrina said as if he had better tell her now.

Scott said settle down young lady your mother is cool. She only went with me because she witnessed me giving that fool my shit.

"Here let me call her for you" Scott start to dial his cellular phone. Scott begun talking "man, put the lady on the phone" then Scott hands Sabrina the phone.

"Hello" the voice on the phone answers, Sabrina respond "Mama?" "Yes" Sabrina? Her mother answers. Sabrina furious Ask her mother "what is going on?" Sabrina mother tell her" I will call you later and talk to you about it" Sabrina tells her mother how worried she was about her and she went with Scott willing.

Sabrina mother told her that there was good money in this for her. Mama but you could have at least let me know you were leaving, I thought something happened to you.

Scott snatch his phone and hung it up, "ok so now you know your mother is ok you better get the fuck out of here" Sabrina did not have to be told twice, she left the club fast not even looking back.

Outside Sabrina saw Bruce in the parking lot and asked why he left the way he did. Bruce told Sabrina because while he was in the men's room, Scott and his boys came in there and told him that Scott saw Bruce with Sabrina and Bruce better leave the club and he meant right then.

Scott told Bruce that he had better hope that he did not leave anything at the table because he was not going back to get it.

That is why I had no chance of telling you I was leaving.

This told Sabrina Scott knew she was in the club all the time. Sabrina just did not know Scott was in the club.

Scott figured that if Bruce went back to the table, Bruce could tell Sabrina that Scott was in the club. Bruce asks Sabrina "what is going on?" because I did not know you were looking for Scott.

Sabrina tell Bruce that she wasn't looking for Scott, so she did not give herself away that she really was there looking for him. Bruce tell Sabrina "let me get out of here because whatever you got going on I don't want to be a part of it"

Bruce walks to his car and left. Sabrina got into her car and left too, once in her car Sabrina drove home and could not wait to call Gail.

# Strung Out

At home Sabrina could not get the door open fast enough, her telephone was ringing as she walked in. running to the telephone Sabrina grab the receiver and answer "hello, it was Gail calling to see if Sabrina was ok. Gail told Sabrina "girl I called several times is everything?"

Sabrina tells Gail about how she spoke with her mother on the telephone, but does not know what is going on. Gail ask "what did you mother say?" Sabrina responds she would not go into details on the telephone, but said that she would call and tell me later.

Sabrina did not know that while she was gone that Gail called around and did some checking on her own. Gail called Michelle and told her what happened at the park.

Michelle told Gail not to get involved because she knew that Sabrina's mother was strung out on drugs. Robert was one of the main people that Sabrina mother get high with. Michelle asks Gail to swear not to tell Sabrina what she just told her.

Gail wanted so badly to tell Sabrina but she had made a promise to Michelle that she would not be involved.

Gail thought back to that incident at the park, this was why Sabrina mother wondered "How Sabrina knew Robert"

Sabrina mother was surprised that Sabrina knew her smoking friend, Sabrina mother never knew that Sabrina knew Robert.

The information was burning inside of Gail and she could not tell her best friend about her mother was so hard. However, the promise that Gail made to her sister, Michelle was more important than Sabrina not knowing about her mother was.

Gary was out of town; Gail called Gary to tell him what was going on and to ask when he would be home. Gary told Gail that she better stay away from Sabrina until all this mess was straightened out.

Gary did not want Gail involved with Sabrina and her mother's drama. Now Gail really had to stay away from Sabrina. First, her sister told her to promise not to tell Sabrina what she said about her, now Gary is telling her that Sabrina is trouble and stay away from her.

Sabrina could not rest with the fact that her mother told her that she would call her and tell her what was going on; Sabrina had to find out for herself.

Sabrina knew people since she worked in a club, so that was where she was going to get information. When Sabrina went to the club, she asked around if any of the girl's knew Robert.

Of course, none of the girl's was going to tell Sabrina if they did, none of the girl's really liked Sabrina at the club. Sabrina had too many enemies at the club.

Every time Sabrina asked anyone, they said no they did not know Robert. Sabrina has a thought to herself "These bitches know Robert".

Sabrina called Gary on his cell phone and asked when he would be home.

Gary asks her why, what is going on? Gary did not tell Sabrina that Gail called and told him the story already. Sabrina told Gary that she missed him and his penis. Gary said "girl why you calling me with that shit?"

He told her that she knew she did not miss him. Sabrina really did not but she wanted some money since she had not been able to return to work.

Gary said, "Ok, I will be back in a few days and I will call you when I'm back" They say their goodbyes and hang up.

Sabrina figure id she wanted to know about Robert then she had to go where Robert hung out…the streets.

Back at the house where Robert and Sabrina mother was at, Scott and his friends were arriving. When Scott went into the house, he saw Robert sitting in a chair and Sabrina's mother was sitting across from him at the table.

Scott looks at Robert and say "ok dude tell me the sorry ass story about why you and this bitch didn't pay me my money" Immediately Sabrina mother tell Scott that she did not know it was his crack that they were smoking.

Scott asks her would it have made a difference if she did. She say yeah, because I know that I did not have any money and I would not fuck with your shit broke.

Scott tell her that all crack heads smoke together and they do not ask where the shit come from. Scott tells her maybe I should get my money from that whore of a daughter of yours, Sabrina.

Sabrina's mother did not want Sabrina to know that she was back smoking crack, so she made a deal with Scott.

Tell you what Scott, if you let me get your money to you next week I promise you will never have to worry about this happening again.

Scott being conceded say "I know this shit won't happen again" Scott had a reputation to uphold; he did not want the guys to see he was soft, so he said to her "bitch, I'll give you the benefit of doubt this time"

You had better have my fucking money or I will get it from you or your daughter. Scott told her that she could leave, Robert got up too. Scott looks at him and asks, "Who said you were dismissed?"

Robert cowardly sat back down and said "I thought" "Yeah I bet you did" Scott interrupting replied.

Scott slaps Robert and tells him to get the fuck out too. Before Robert got to the door Scott told him "you better make sure you and that bitch have my money in seven days and I don't mean eight days either.

Robert left the house so fast until he nearly fell down the stairs outside as he went down them. Sabrina's mother did not get far; she was around the corner when Robert walked down the street.

She jumped out around the corner right into Robert's path. She asked "Why didn't you tell me that was Scott's shit, man?"

Robert said shut the fuck up, you enjoyed it as well as I did. They laughed but Robert we have to get Scott's money, she said after laughing.

Robert said "fuck Scott he don't scare me" She told Robert well I am getting his money and giving it to him.

I will not be fucking with you any more because you will get a bitch killed Sabrina mother walk away to a telephone so she could call Sabrina to tell her to come take her home.

# Street Tricking

Sabrina mother dialed Sabrina number, the phone rung but there was not an answer. Her mother curse as she hung the phone receiver up "where in the funk can that girl be" she begun walking toward her house.

Sabrina was on the telephone calling to see if Gary got home yet. Sabrina called Gary's phone and he answers, "What's up Ms. Lady?"

Sabrina asks are you home yet? Gary tells her that he said he would call her. Damn, Sabrina says aloud and Gary asks her "what's going on?"

Sabrina told him that she wanted to hook up with him that is all. Gary tells her "oh don't worry, because we have to talk" We do. About what Sabrina ask with curiosity.

Well do you want to wait until I get back for me to tell you, or do you want to know now? Gary replied with an "it do not matter to me voice"

Sabrina laughs but not like it was funny laugh. She hesitantly tells Gary that he could tell her now. Gary tell Sabrina that he knew a couple of months ago she gave him a STD.

Sabrina defensibly asks, "What the fuck you talking about I gave you a STD?" Gary say "look it's ok now but girl you better watch who you give that pussy to. Sabrina still pretending not to know what Gary was talking about, she tell him "I 'm clean and I did not have an STD".

Gary tells her that he is not mad at her but if he gives Gail something like that, she is going to kill him. Well Gary you call me when you get in town. Gary told her ok then hung the phone up.

When Sabrina got to the street she look around and there were so many people walking around like it was a parade. Some of the people were standing in the doorways and the others were just walking back and forth.

The park across the street actually had tents pitched up as it was a campground but this is where those people lived…inside the tents in the park.

There were many girls trying to get a date from the cars that passed by. Some of the girls were hollering while shaking their asses and pulling up their skirts.

Sabrina was looking so hard at what was going on until she did not notice her mother waving her arms for her to turn the car around.

Her mother ran across the street and jumped into the car, "damn girl I called you so much until I was about to give up then you answered" Sabrina proceeded to drive her mother home when she asked her what is going on with her and Robert.

Sabrina mother told her that Robert owed Scott money for some crack that he got. Sabrina quickly asks her "please tell me that you haven't started back smoking?"

Her mother stares out the window, not looking in Sabrina's direction. Sabrina asks well. Her mother say well what?

Mama you have! You started back didn't you? Sabrina asks. Sabrina you do not understand, that monkey is hard to shake, her mother replied. However, mama all you had to do is come to me and we could have worked it out.

Sabrina, you are not always, around when I need you, her mother insisted. The club takes all your time when I need you, Sabrina's mother said while she was trying to run a quilt trip on her. When Sabrina and her mother got to the house Sabrina insisted on coming inside with her.

Sabrina wanted to finish the conversation about why she started back using the crack. This was the last thing that her mother wanted to talk about, because she was not ready to stop her use.

Sabrina told her that she was coming in the house for a minute or two, but her mother did not want her to come in. She had other plans like how she was going to get Scott money.

Sabrina mother made up an excuse as if she was tired and wanted to lay down to take a nap. Sabrina knew her mother was making up the excuse but how could she prove it, so she left.

Sabrina was not off the block good enough before her mother was on the phone calling around trying to set up a date. She knew she needed to get some money for Scott as well as she wanted to some money for herself; she wanted to get another hit of crack.

She called and called but she could not get anyone that was willing to come over. Her only solution now was to go where the money was, back on the street.

She got herself all made up, and then put on a dress that looks as if it could have been a t-shirt.

She headed out the door and down the street to the corner by the drug store.

She was not alone, there were several girls on the street with the same idea as she had, some of the girls were there for their pimps and others were there to support their drug habits.

Sabrina called Gail while driving home to tell her the she thinks her mother is back using crack. Sabrina told Gail "If my mother is using that shit again, she will be in rehabilitation so fast until it's going to make her head swim"

Gail ask Sabrina why do you think she is using again? Sabrina said because when she asked her mother if she was using, her mother did not answer her. She just stared out of the window.

At that point she started to talk about how bad the monkey was on her back, if that was not admitting she was using in so many words I don't know what would, Sabrina replies.

Gail wanted so badly to tell Sabrina that she knew her mother was using but because of the promise Gail made to Michelle, she could not tell Sabrina.

Gail figured since Sabrina was calling her with the story then Sabrina had an idea already. Gail sat waiting on Gary to come home; this was the day that Gary said that he would be home.

Gail told Sabrina that she could not sit on the phone to long because she had to get the house in order.

"What you mean, get the house in order?" Sabrina asks. Gail said because Gary is coming home girl and I need to be ready.

Sabrina thought to herself, Gary ass did not tell me that he would be home today. Sabrina told Gail "oh ok girl, you go ahead and get that stuff together, I will talk to you later"

Back on the street Sabrina mother was turning tricks with the local John's coming in the neighborhood looking for girls. Sabrina mother had made enough money for her to get a rock to smoke but she then was working on getting Scott's money.

Sabrina mother was so high until when she went back out she was too high to make enough money for the debt that she owed to Scott.

She was totally out her of her head and did not know what she was doing. She walked into the store because she was thirsty but she did not have any money, she had plans on stealing a beer.

The store cashier was watching her in the mirror that is mounted at the end of the aisle. She went to the cooler and picked up a beer then she put the beer underneath her shirt.

As she attempt to walk out, the man grabbed her by the arm and asked "Hey aren't you going to pay for the beer?"

During the struggle of trying to free herself before she got the words out that she did not have a beer, the beer fell from her shirt and hit the floor.

She looked at him and told him that she did not have any money, the man told her to get the fuck out of the store. In addition, if she came back in there he would crack her upside her head.

She had another idea on how she would get a beer, she thought about standing outside of the store because surely on of the drunks outside would share their drink with her.

Some people walk pass and she asked if she could have their change when they came out of the store.

One of the men said "Hell nah, get a job" she took offence to this and told him to kiss her ass. He turn and ask "what you say bitch?" His friends laughed, but restrain him from approaching her.

The other people tell him to leave her alone that he could see that she was not anything but a crack head trying to get up on another rock. He told them that he did not care, was not no bitch going to tell him to kiss her ass and get away with it.

They hurried him into the store and she walked away because she did not know what the man would do to her if she stood around.

Friend or Foe


At Gail's house she was cleaning and cooking, excited
that, Gary would soon be home. The mail carrier
dropped the mail through the slot in the door; Gail
heard the mail drop through the door and thought it was
Gail coming in.

One envelope that came was from Gary's cellular
company, the letter was very thick, thicker then usual
and it made a thump when it hit the floor.

Gail usually did not open Gary's mail but she wanted to
know why the envelope was so thick. Gail knew if the
envelope was thick that it meant that the bill had
multiple pages, she wanted to see whom Gary was
calling.

Gail was a person that wrote down dates to everything,
she lived off her notes from her journal. So begun to
open the envelope when the door bell rung.

Gail put the envelope under the sofa pillow, and then
proceeded to the door, she open it to find it was
Michelle.

Michelle asked Gail what she had up for the day. Gail
with the look of "I'm up to something" told Michelle
nothing. Michelle then asked Gail "what were you
doing? Because I know that look" Gail said nothing.

Michelle said, "Come on now Gail, I know you and you
were doing something" Gail laughing said ok, but you
had better not say anything. Say nothing about what?
Michelle asks.

Gail go under the sofa pillow and pull out Gary's mail, Gail tell Michelle that Gary's cell phone just came and she wanted to see who he was calling.

Ms. Eager Michelle was excited to know herself, because she was the one that always said Gary was a cheater.

Michelle did not have any facts that Gary cheated but Michelle way of saying it, all men cheat. They rush to open it, then Gail pause "maybe I shouldn't be doing this" Gail said as if to be having second thought about opening it.

Radical Michelle said "and maybe you should" Gail say ok then rip the envelope open, the first page consist of numbers when Gary called home and his job.

The second page was numbers that Gail did not know but none of the numbers repeated themselves. Each number, the conversation was only for a minute or two.

Then Michelle took a page of numbers, as she look over the page she say "oh my GOD!" Gail wanted to know what Michelle saw.

She asked what is it? Michelle responds, "There are multiple times that Gary called and talked for some time to this number"

Michelle said the number look familiar, but how would I know whom Gary is calling? Gail tells Michelle to hand her the paper and show her what number she was talking about.

Michelle pointed out the number and the times he called it. Gail say "girl that's Sabrina's number" Michelle say it is. Why is he calling her so much?

Gail said good question but I am sure he had his reasons; maybe he was looking for David.

Michelle say yeah but maybe he was looking for Sabrina. Gail told Michelle "there you go again with your Sherlock idea's"

Gail goes on to tell Michelle that she knew that Sabrina is her best friend and if she trusted anybody with Gary besides Michelle it would be Sabrina.

Michelle ask "but aren't you at least curious to know why they talk so much?" You know what, to satisfy that mind I will ask him when he get here, ok?

Michelle had her way of being a smart ass too, she told Gail" if you ask or not I won't know, but if he was my husband that shit would cease, best friends or not"

Hell, I was always told pussy don't have a face and dick don't have a conscious, this was Michelle's way of telling Gail don't trust Sabrina or Gary. Michelle said without being descriptive, why don't you call and ask Sabrina about the calls?

You know what? That's what I'll do, if it will shut you up. Gail got the telephone and dialed Sabrina's number. The telephone continued to ring but as Gail start to hang it up David answers.

"Hello" was David respond, Hi David is Sabrina around? Gail asks. David tell Gail no she went to the store, is there something that you want me to tell her?

Michelle was in the background insisting Gail tell David about the calls. David asks, "Is that Michelle I hear in the background?"

In addition, what is she so excited about? Gail say "it's nothing, Michelle yells out "yes it is David" David heard Michelle and asked what's going on?

Michelle snatches the phone from Gail and tells David that Sabrina's cell number is on Gary's phone bill several times and they were trying to figure out why. David was angry about what he just heard but wanted to keep his composure about it.

David asks to speak back to Gail, so Michelle hand Gail the phone back. "Gail let's keep this hush-hush until I do a little research on it ok?" David asked.

Gail asks David do you think there is something to this. David responds he is not certain but he want to find out his way, so do not mention this to Gary or Sabrina. Gail tells David ok then hangs up the phone.

Gail looks at Michelle and asks "What did we just do? What did we just do? Michelle said with the look on her face as if to say "their the one's that fucked up"

Gail ask Michelle "honestly, do you think that they are messing around?" Michelle told her that she really do not know but they have a lot of explaining to do.

Why else would Gary and Sabrina be talking so much to each other and Gail and David not know about it, Michelle thought.

Gail was so upset until she told Michelle, I should call Gary right now and ask him what is going on. David asked me to wait for whatever reason he had, but I want to know now.

The way it sound to me David had some suspicion already, he just want to play it cool for now.

Gail yells out with fury "how could she? How could they? Michelle knew Gail was upset so she tried to calm her down by saying "we are assuming now , Gail "

Nothing has been proven yet. That's true Michelle but why all the calling like you said? Gail why don't you call Gary and ask for yourself so you don't be so upset.

I want to call him but shouldn't I wait like David asked? Gail asked with uncertainty. If Gary was my husband and Sabrina was my friend if I thought the two of them were messing around, I wouldn't want to wait, I couldn't wait to find out, so call Gary.

Gail was easily influenced, she followed Michelle's advice and called Gary. But she questioned "how would she ask him about the calls without upsetting him"

Michelle said who give a fuck if he is upset, the cheating bastard. Maybe you should say the hell with him and go get fucked by someone else and let him find out.

See how he would like that. Michelle maybe I should wait, but I'm so angry until if Gary was here I might slap his fucking face, Gail said as she hung the phone back up.

Michelle sighs "girl you are one scary ass, I would call fuck that!" Gail tell Michelle that she is going to take a nap, all of this gave her a headache.

 Michelle said well I'm leaving but I will call you later so you can tell me you did not find the nerve to call him, laughing as she walk out the door.

Gail don't have the nerve to call Gary but she and Sabrina were suppose to be friends so instead she called her. Gail dialed Sabrina and she answers "what's up girly?" Sabrina ask with excitement.

Gail didn't even respond to Sabrina question instead she blares out "Girl you fucking Gary?"

"What the fuck!" was Sabrina's response to the accusation, why would you call me with that shit? What ever gave you that idea?

Gail lowers her tone and say "but I saw Gary's phone bill and your number is on the bill several times"

Girl, David and I are having problems and I been asking Gary for his advice. "Oh, shit I feel like a total fool now, I'm sorry Sabrina" Was Gail's respond back to Sabrina.

And I thought you and I were home girls, but you thought I wanted your man? What kind of friend are you, Gail?

Sabrina asked while covering the fact that she was the wrong one here.

Gail felt bad enough accusing her friend of wanting her man but now Sabrina convinced her she was wrong.

Gail offers her apology again but Sabrina play it off by telling Gail that she would talk to her later, she needed time to think about this and hung up the phone.

Gail thought that she had made a terrible mistake and now she knew she better call Gary because she wanted to call him before Sabrina did.

Meanwhile Sabrina did call Gary just to give him the head's up on Gail might know something. When

Sabrina called she told Gary about Gail's call to her, he wanted to know what was said and what did Sabrina tell Gail.

Sabrina told Gary that she assured Gail that nothing was going on but that she was calling Gary for advice because she and David were having problems.

Gary sarcastically said " you and David are having problems, he don't fuck you like I do"

Sabrina said " funny, but you better remember what I said, so if Gail call you then you know what to say" Gary told Sabrina that he knew how to handle Gail if she called. Gary and Sabrina hung the telephone up.

# Rendezvous

David could not wait to find out what was going on with Sabrina and Gary. He always had his suspicions about Gary looking at Sabrina as if he wanted her, and now this.

David told himself "I knew that muthafucker Gary wanted my wife" Let me find out that they were messing around I will beat Gary's ass, was all David kept thinking.

David knew Sabrina was like cheap mayonnaise, spread easy. He did not care that he met her in the club but to think of Gary having his way with her was out of the question.

Whore or not to David Sabrina was his whore as he expressed it to the fellows when he met her, but now she is his wife.

Things are different now, he knew some of the fellows teased and said "You can't make a whore a housewife"

David was characterized in the neighborhood as a player. David kept his bachelor ways but he tried to make Sabrina retire hers.

Everyone knew technically Sabrina was not a whore because she was fucking free half the time, and whores get paid.

Sabrina mother called her and she wanted her to come over to her house.

Sabrina made plans to meet with Josh, so her mother call helped her get out of the house.

But she knew she was not trying to go over there. David thought Sabrina was going to her mother's house when she left but Sabrina was on her way to meet Josh.

Sabrina was on the phone with Josh once she got into her truck. "Hey where are you? Sabrina asked. Josh replied "waiting to tap that ass" Sabrina laughs.

Sabrina then tells Josh he had better make it worth her while. Josh chauvinistically say "I will make you forget who your man is"

Sabrina sighs " damn you got this pussy wet and throbbing" Josh tell her not to get a speeding ticket on the way but hurry.

Sabrina respond to Josh by telling him just have the dick ready. Sabrina call her mother back to let her know that she need to make a stop before she come over, but if David call tell him that she ran some errands for her.

David was smarter than Sabrina thought, he was planning to follow her. So when she left the house she did not realize David was behind her in his car.

David had to stay behind Sabrina a couple of cars so she could not see him. Traffic was heavy, as usual, I-94 was bumper to bumper.

Sabrina weaved in and out of the lanes, making David distance between the two of them wider and wider. Her sporadic driving caught the attention of the state police car that was on the grass beside the ramp behind her.

She never saw him because she was too occupied talking shit to Josh on the telephone. Down the ramp the police car came, David had to merge to let the officer into traffic.

Damn it, the bitch is being pulled over David said.
Sabrina looked through the rear view mirror and all she
could see were the disco lights dancing.

Therefore, she pulled to the side to let the police get by
but instead he pulled behind her. "What the fuck?" he is
getting behind me Sabrina realized.

The officer got out of his patrol car; Sabrina thought,
"Good I will get out of this after she saw that it was a
man officer"

She fixes her breasts, opening her blouse so that the
breast stood up like plumb melons.

Fixing her hair as the officer stood just behind the
opening to the driver's door.

"Ms. what's the hurry?" the officer asks. Sabrina lean over the door, breast hanging forward about to pop out the blouse.

"Was I going fast officer? She ask as she suddenly bite her lip sensually, the officer notice her breast but try not to make it obvious. He asks her for her license, registration and proof of insurance.

Now the officer is more in front of the driver's door, allowing himself a straight view of the melons. Sabrina knew he was looking so she made the breast jiggle with every movement.

Looking through her wallet she got the documents he asked for, she handed them to him. He never left the car door, he look at them and hand them back to her.

Sabrina confidence just kicked into extreme, she got him where she wants him to be, under her control. He look at her and tell her "Ms you "breast" um um excuse me correcting himself say better be careful and slow down"

He turn and walk away returning to his car get in and pull off. She laughs as she say "Sucker ass mother fucker"

Meanwhile, David had to continue driving pass so now he was well in front of Sabrina. His plans did not work out well; because the first exit Sabrina got to, she got off the expressway.

Sabrina still entertaining the thought about being with Josh drives and parks her truck around the corner. She walks up to Josh house and rung the bell, Josh come to the door with just a towel around his waist.

Josh was about to shower when Sabrina rung the bell, Josh opens the door and Sabrina stood looking him up and down. Sabrina looks at Josh chest and say" Damn, I never knew you had all that"

Josh exercised regularly and his chest was well formed, his abdomen had an eight-pack muscle formation. I knew you were cut up but damn you look good, Sabrina told Josh.

Josh blushing grabs Sabrina through the door closing the door with his foot. As the door close the towel drops, Sabrina was astound, Josh was nowhere near Gary's size.

Josh was truly blessed, as Sabrina would describe it. Josh embrace Sabrina as he press against her letting her feel the hardness of his manhood.

His hand slide underneath her blouse allowing him to feel the firmness of her now erect nipples. Josh drop to his knee's placing his head between Sabrina's thighs, removing her g-string with his teeth.

He continue to explore Sabrina thighs with his tongue, Sabrina is now in the come and get it mode. Sabrina lean against the wall, sliding down onto the floor with Josh attached to her clitoris.

She was so into felling how Josh was working his magical tongue until at this moment she was passing the stars on her way to the moon.

Sabrina moaned with each flicker of Josh tongue. Touchdown, Sabrina reach climax. She releases a sensual scream of passion.

Sabrina knew she was hooked at this moment and did not think about her original plans of getting Josh money.

She thought if Josh continue to eat pussy the way that he does, then she would use him for the sex and Gary for the money and let Gary keep his little ass penis.

Sabrina thought to herself without saying it "Damn the boy can work magic with his tongue" Josh was better than David ever was, hell he was better than anyone Sabrina had.

Sabrina pussy still throbbing, she sat up and leaned over grasping Josh penis in one hand while her tongue slid down one side of it. She circled the rim of the head slowly, nibbling the head ever so gently.

This was driving Josh wild, the penis hardened until the vain pulsated uncontrollably. Sabrina covered the penis while she slid it in and out of her mouth fast then slow, back and forth.

Josh could not handle much more of this; she placed the penis in between her breast while she made jerking motions. Josh climaxes as Sabrina stroked the penis jerking it off with her hand.

The thick creamy orgasm ran down Sabrina breast onto her stomach. She picked up the towel that Josh came to the door in and wiped the orgasm from herself.

Josh lay still on his back and dozed off, Sabrina did not mind because she knew that she really whipped the pussy on him.

The dancer's from the club told her if after sex a man fall asleep then the pussy he got must have been good.

Sabrina was whipped because she lay on the other side of Josh and fell asleep herself.

# Watchful Eyes

Sabrina wake up to the sound of her phone ringing, quickly she picks it up to see not just, who was calling but to see what time it was.

Sabrina saw that it was her mother calling and answered. "Hello Mama" Sabrina said "Sabrina where are you?" I have been expecting you for hours; David called and said that he was on his way over here, so you had better get over here her mother said.

Sabrina got up, waking Josh with her movement. Josh asked where she was going as if he thought she was spending the night with him.

Sabrina replied that she had to hurry over to her mothers before David got there. Josh wondered if when her phone rung it was David calling.

Sabrina did not volunteer to say who it was on the phone but Josh knew by the way that Sabrina was hurrying that it was someone telling her she had better be where David thought she was.

Sabrina hurried and left, Josh was trying to walk her to the door but Sabrina was out the door before Josh could get up.

Sabrina hurried to her truck, calling her mother back on the way, her mother questioned her where she was but of course, Sabrina would not tell that she was coming from Josh house.

Her mother asked her why she had to be so damn secretive all the time; Sabrina told her that she is a grown woman.

Secrets had nothing to do with it if she did not want her to know where she was. "If I don't want to tell you where I'm at or going I have that right," Sabrina said trying not to sound disrespectful.

Her mother got offended but did not say anything; she asked Sabrina how long it would be before she got over there.

Sabrina told her that she was less than five minutes away, but why the big concern. Her mother reminded her that David was on his way to her house and she wanted Sabrina to get there first.

Sabrina told her if David get there before she did for her to tell him that she went to the store. "Sabrina you better stop and buy something then, her mother replied.

Sabrina knowing her mother knew she wanted something from the store so she asked her what she wanted.

Her mother laughs but told her to buy her a beer, Sabrina asks, "What size do you want?" Her mother say well since you asked, bring me a forty ounce.

Sabrina laughs and say to her "Mama you are something else" ok I am at the store so I will be there as soon as I leave here.

Her mother hang up the phone in time enough to answer the door, which David was there knocking. As she opened the door, she acted as if she was surprised to see him.

"Hey David" what is going on? She asks. David replied not much, where is Sabrina because her truck was not outside.

Sabrina mother was glad that Sabrina already told her what to say to David if he came and she was not there.

She responded "Oh, she went to the store to get me a beer" David sat down and begun to watch television but he checked his watch from time to time to see how long if would be before Sabrina got back.

Sabrina walk into the door, she act as if she was there all the time but as her mother said just went to the store. Acting surprised to see David she ask him what he was doing there.

David told her that he was bored at the house so he decided to come over there with them. Sabrina did not trust David and he did not trust her, David knew she was up to something but just could never catch her.

Sabrina was the one that no one could trust but she was slick with her shit. At least she thought she was, as long as she got away with her sneaking.

David was determined to catch Sabrina up to something, he knew he really did not want to know but his curiosity was getting the best of him.

Sabrina had everyone fooled, she was acting as she was innocent but she was out for her own selfish personal gain.

She would go to the beauty salon and tell the girls how she could work a guy to get his money but little did she know that one day her mouth was what her trouble was.

She did not know how to keep it shut, she talked too much and to the wrong people.

Sabrina mother told her why she wanted her to come over but since David was there he might as well knew too.

She confessed that she begun smoking crack again and now owed Scott money. She and Robert smoked his crack; she did not know that it was Scott's crack.

Now Scott wants his money for it and she does not have enough to pay him back.

"What am I going to do?" She asked David and Sabrina. Sabrina looks at David and asks him if he has money,

David asks Sabrina mother how much you owe him. Initially she look to the floor then she say Scott said that it was three hundred dollars.

Three hundred? Are you serious? David asked as if she was crazy if she thought that he would pay a three hundred dollar drug debt.

Fuck! I do not even smoke and you think that I would pay that to a thug, David reaction infers.

Sabrina in a calm voice ask David so what can she do? David pace the floor thinking "let me think" he replied.

David said let me talk to Scott and I will come up with something. Sabrina assure her mother to let David handle it, he will take care of it.

However, whatever you do, you better laid low for a couple of days until David fix this. David told Sabrina that it was time for them to go home, Sabrina tell her mother that she will call her later and they left.

David and Sabrina get into their vehicles and drive home, at the house David ask Sabrina how do your mother get herself into so much trouble.

Sabrina told him that she had no idea but this time she was over her head, fucking with Scott and his gang.

Scott is the most treacherous man that she had ever met, and she knew many of no good people. Sabrina asked David what were his plans on handling Scott.

David did not have an immediate answer but he knew he had to do something and it had to be soon because there was no telling how long her mother had to get Scott money to him.

David did remember that Sabrina's mother mentioned Robert, saying that the both of them owed Scott, so he wanted to see how money Robert had towards this debt.

David asked Sabrina do you know where Robert could be found. Sabrina said not really but some one on the street could direct them to him she was sure.

David and Sabrina got into David car and drove to where she thought she could find Robert, near the park.

Once at the park they asked around to see if anyone knew where Robert could be found. After asking people, they were told that he live downtown near Hart plaza in an apartment building.

The man did not know the address but described the building to them and told them how they could get there.

They drove down Linwood on their way downtown to find Robert. Sabrina knew that someone would know Robert because he was from this area and everyone knew him.

David was upset that he had to be out look for a crack head, when he could have been at home in comfort.

They drove towards Hart Plaza, they begun looking for the apartment that man described. They saw so many buildings that could possibly be the building.

All these building were well maintained so they did not think this was where Robert lived since he was a crack head, but David told Sabrina that they could not go off that.

Robert could be a closet smoker, well maintained but still smoked. Sabrina agreed because she knew that some of the girls at the club got down like that but if you did not see them smoke, you would not know it.

David park at this one building and asked some of the people outside if Robert lived there and they told him that he did not. So David continued on to the next building.

This building was not as well kept as the first building was but it still was livable. David again gets out of the car only to be told no Robert did not live there either.

Damn, where is the fool David questioned as he got back into the car. Sabrina tells him to have patience because someone down here knows him and we will find him.

David angrily tell her "here we are looking for a damn crack head and your mother is sitting back drinking fucking beer in the comfort of her home"

We should be at home fucking doing what we wanted or whatever but no, we have to find Mr. I will smoke now and pay you later. Sabrina told David to go closer to Hart Plaza which is where the man said the building was, so David drove closer to Hart Plaza.

They come to another building and David tell Sabrina "this is the last building that he would go to then he's going home, fuck they would never find Robert"

Outside the building look clean but it was obvious that it was barely being kept up. Sabrina insisted that this had to be the building; David asks, "How can you be so sure?"

Sabrina said because didn't you see those women on the other side; they look like they had just turned a trick or looking to turn one. This had to be the one Sabrina insisted or she was being hopeful because she knew David was not looking any further if this was not.

Both David and Sabrina got out this time because Sabrina was tired of looking too; she wanted to go home just as bad as David did.

They walk up to the building; no one was outside besides the women that Sabrina saw on the side. They look at the residence listing on the wall.

There was a R. Tolbert, Sabrina said let us try it. David rung the bell but there was no answer. Damn after all this, now the fucker is not at home if in fact this is he on the listing board.

Before leaving Sabrina suggested David, ring the manager's bell to see if this is, Robert's building. David rung the bell "who is it?" a voice come over the speaker asking.

"Hello" my name is David, my wife and I was looking for Robert. Can you tell me if he lives here? The voice does not answer.

David and Sabrina look at one another, then at the door leading inside the hallway stood a little woman. She slowly opened the door looking around to see who was standing outside.

She invites them in "come on in" now what were you saying she asks. We were wondering if Robert lived in this building David asks.

"Well there is a Robert on the third floor but I have not seen him in a couple of days" the woman said. Do you

want to go up to see if he is here? She asked. Sabrina
say why not since you went through the trouble of
opening the door that would the least we could do.

She lead them to the elevator and they all enter, the
elevator was one of the evelator's that you had to close
the iron gate yourself before closing the door.

The door shut and the evelator starts to make its
movement, finally coming to a stop on the second floor.

As the door opens and outside in the hall way stood and
woman and her man for the evening, the woman
greeted Ramona, whom was with David and Sabrina.

"Hello Ramona, what's up with you?" the woman said
as she and the man enters the elevator.

Ramona replied not much as if she really did not have
much to say to the woman. She closes the elevator door
and continues to the third floor.

As the elevator came to a stop, Ramona open the door
and everyone including the woman and her friend exits.

The woman and her man friend go into her apartment
down the hall, as the door closes they could hear her
giggling like a schoolchild.

Ramona came to apartment two zero eight the door
where Robert lived, she knock but there was not an
answer.

Ramona has the master key so she took it upon herself to open the door.

David and Sabrina questioned should they be going into Robert's apartment if he was not at home, Ramona told them she was the owner and she could go in if she felt like it.

Ramona open the door and she look around; there was a smell in the apartment like no one had ever smelled before. Ramona run to the window opening it as she asked "what the fuck is that smell?"

That shit smell like something is dead; David and Sabrina covering their noses walk back out the apartment while Ramona was still trying to find where the smell was coming from.

Ramona walk down the hallway leading to Robert's bedroom, the smell was getting stronger. She opens the door, the room was dark but it was obvious that the smell was coming from the room.

Ramona turns the light on and she found the smell, Robert was lying on the floor next to the bed.

Ramona call from David to come in the apartment, David followed the sound of her voice into the room where he too now seen Robert lying on the floor.

David asks, "Is he…." Ramona said very much so. Sabrina is now coming down the hall and David tells her to go back out to the hallway.

Sabrina ask what is going on, David walk out to where Sabrina was and told her that Robert was dead in the apartment.

Ramona now in the hallway with them ask them to call the police. Sabrina ask David did it look as if Robert was killed.

David say no Robert had a crack pipe lying next to him;
he must have gotten the ultimate high.

The police came and ask questions, they had to stay at the apartment for three hours until they find out what happened to Robert. Sabrina calls her mother and told her what they just came across and she was worried that Scott had something to do with it.

She told her mother to leave her house and go to Gail and Gary's until they pick her up because she was not chancing Scott and his friends.

Until Scott had his money, Sabrina did not want her mother to be left alone.

# Suspicions

Finally, David and Sabrina were able to go home and they were more than happy about it.Sabrina's mother glad to see them, she could not wait to find out what happened to Robert.

David was just glad to be home and the ordeal about Robert was behind him.David let Sabrina know that he would pay Scott for her mother but she had to leave, she could not stay at their house.

Meanwhile Michelle was on the telephone trying to hook up with Josh for the night.Michelle was on a night creep, Josh was not really in the mood for this because Sabrina already set him straight.

Michelle was being persistant because she knew Josh was packing and she yarned for that. It was no surprise to her, Sabrina was just finding out why Michelle always smiled when Josh came around.

Josh gave into Michelle persistence and allowed her to come over but Michelle thought it was going to be for other reasons, she did not know that Sabrina left Josh less then an hour ago.

Gail wanted Gary to take her on a vacation, away from the neighborhood. She sadi that she was tired of just sitting in the house but Gary had just gotten back from a business trip and wanted to saty home.

Michelle was whispering in Gail's ear every chance she got, Gail never complaint like this before the phone bill came but since she suspected Gary of cheating although Sabrina tried to assure her if Gary was cheating it was not with her, Gail want Gary to spend more time with her.

Gary was wondering why the sudden change in Gail but he did not know it was Micheel that was building Gail up to question Gary.

Gary asked Gail why she opened his mail any way; Gail told him what did he have to hide.

Gary told her if he was hiding something then the bill would not have came to the house to begin with, he would have send it somewhere else.

Gary and Gail never argued like their were now and Michelle had her own reasoning for it, she told Gail if Gary want to create a argument with you now, it's because he is fucking someone else.

Gary did not know that Gail was starting to watch him closer by writing down times he was on the phone, how long or when he left and how long he was gone. She kept notes inside of her journal so she could look back on certain days and compare it to what she wrote in the journal.

This made Gail wonder because she and Sabrina were not as close as they once was, Gail wondered were Sabrina and Gary cheating or was it because of the accusation Gail made towards Sabrina.

Gary demands that Gail not talk about his telephone bill anymore especially sice Gail wanted to mention Sabrina's name in the conversation.

Gary told Gail that he did not appreciate her tone, or her words towards him, Gail told Gary "And I don't like the idea that my husband and my best friend might be fucking one another"

Gary could not say to much more because he knew deep inside Gail was right with what she said, he just could not admit to it. Gail would kill them both if she knew or could prove it.

Gary idea was since he was in town he could later sneak and call Sabrina.He just wanted to first wait and let Gail settle down but the first chance he got he was out the house and back with Sabrina.

A lot had changed since Gary was gone Sabrina had her mark on Josh because he had the money and what Sabrina wanted.

David in the meanwhile was so busy watching Sabrina so she would not get with Gary until Josh slid right in under his nose and was fucking Sabrina.

Gail determined to watch Gary hired an investigator that would get her the information she needed to prove Gary was a cheater.

She did not know what she would find out from the investigation.

Gail called David back to see how he was coming along with his plans to see if Gary and Sabrina were messing around.

David angry about Sabrina's mother ordeal lash out at Gail, when he answered the phone he let it be known.

Damn Gail why do you insist on asking me questions about rather your fucking husband is banging my wife? David asks.

Gail told David "hey you are the one that said wait and you would do your own investigation"

David later tell Gail that he meant no harm but he has a situation going on at the house that really have him in turmoil.

Gail wanted to know if she could be of any help, strictly, because that was her way of finding out what was going on. She really did not want to help

David but if he told her yes she could help then she would know what was going on.

David not realizing what Gail was doing told her everything. David told her that Sabrina crack head ass mother and her friend Robert owed Scott money for drug that they smoked.

Gail asks so why don't the two of them pay him back and how does that have any effect on him. David goes on to say because Robert was found dead and she don't have shit but the drug debt.

Sabrina got the bitch living here with us until I pay Scott the money as if I smoked his shit. Gail reply "Damn now I see why you would be uptight"

Why doesn't Sabrina pay Scott back? Gail ask, David tell her Sabrina have not went back to work yet so she do not have any money.

Gail told David her plans of hiring an investigator for Gary and David agree that it might work. He tells her that it is not a bad idea and that he wants the man to follow Sabrina also.

Gail tells David to call the man and talk to him, that she was sure that he would love the extra work.

David call the man and he agree to follow Sabrina but first David had to take her picture to the man's office downtown.

David let him know that it would not be a problem; he would bring a picture today if he wanted. The man told David the sooner the better, because he could get on the case right away.

David told him ok I will be at your office in the afternoon.David called Gail back and askd if she wanted to join him to meet with the man.

Gail let him know that she had other things to do around the house so she could not go. Gary walks into the house and he wonder who Gail is talking too.

Gail tells David without saying his name that she would call his back later, David agrees and they hang up.

Gary asks Gail "so who was that on the phone?" Gail knew she could not say David but instead she say, "Oh that was Michelle"

Gail hurry out the room only so Gary could not continue to question her. The telephone rung, Gary and Gail only had the one phone and it is in the room where Gary is.

Gary answers "Hello" the voice in the telephone respond, "Hello, Gary is Gail home?" Gary ask who is calling, the woman said Gary it is I Michelle.

Dang girl did you forget something? Gary asks. Michelle asks Gary what he meant, not knowing that Gail just said that she was just talking to her.

Gary say you stay on the phone calling here don't you?

Michelle tell him shut the fuck up this was her first time she called Gail today.Gary say "I am not talking about the time that Gail called you earlier, Michelle still not thinking say but I have not spoke with Gail today.

Gary said oh I am sorry I thought you two talked today, Michelle tell him that he is so damn crazy so get off the phone and get Gail if she is home.

Gary call Gail to tell her that Michelle is on the phone,Gail thought to herself "fuck" Michelle had bad timing this time now Gary knew Gail was talking to someone else and it was not Michelle, so who was she talking to and why did she lie about who it was.

Since Michelle did call there was no way Gary could hit *69 because it would ring back to Michelle because she was the last caller. Gail came back into the room and pick up the phone, Michelle tell her that she wss spending the night at Josh house and that she was turning her phone off if Gail wanted her to call Josh's house.

Gail told Michelle ok and they hung the phone up. Gail tried to leave back out of the room but not before Gary stops her and ask, "Is there something that you want to say to me?"

Gail pretends not to know what Gary meant. "What you mean, she asks. Gary said when I came home you where on the phone and I asked whom you were talking too, you said it was Michelle. Michelle just told me that she had not talked with you today.

Gail what is going on? Gary asked with a look on his face of anger.Gail stood looking dumb, like what the fuck can I say that would possibly get me out of this shit.

David was on his way to the investigator's office downtown to take Sabrina picture to him. David parks his car in front of the building and goes in.

David got a ticket as soon as he left the car, when he walks inside. David goes to the investigator office and his receptionist tells David to have a seat.

Shortly the investigator tells his receptionist to send David in his office. David gets up and walks into the room where the investigator was.

Sitting behind the desk was a man that appeared to be in his early fifty's with salt and pepper hair. The man rose as David approached the desk.

With his hand extended out for a handshake he told David welcome, now explain to me why you think that your wife is cheating and again whom do you think it is with.

David tell the investigator that he think it is Gary Halsey, the investigator look up toward the ceiling and say wait that's the woman that called me earlier husband right?

Therefore, you and the woman think that your spouses are cheating with one another. David said exactly, So do you think that you could find out for us? David wants to know.

The investigator assures David that he has been doing this kind of work for thirty-five years and if his wife Sabrina were having an affair then he would be the one to know it.

David tell him find, but it is of the ulmost importance that you tell me first. I know Gail hired you first, but I want to handle this before Gail knows, ok David ask.

David add another hundred dollars for his troubles, really David knew he was paying to get the first information before Gail.

However, between men David told him that if he did not tell Gail what he asked, David definitely would not.

The investigator told David no problem bud, David say good enough, how soon can you start? The investigator tell David I will be starting today, you paid me today didn't you?

David left and took the ticket from his windshield, he drove home and Sabrina was gone.David wondered wher could she possibly be, he figured that she would be gone when he got home because that was her opportunity to leave when he wa gone , so he would not be there to ask her where she was going.

Sabrina was at the beauty salon getting her hair done when her phone rung.It was David asking wher she was.
Sabrina told his where she was and he told her to call him when she left.

Sabrina hung up the phone but she then start to talk to the girls in the shop about how jealous David was.

She was talking too much because David friends' girl was in the shop and Sabrina had never met her. She only knew Sabrina by the way the other girls in the salon addressed "here come the whore of the neighborhood, when they saw Sabrina coming"

Sabrina conitnue on how she was the shit because she was fucking Gary and his friend Josh and milking them both of money.Some of the girl laughed but others did not, because they knew Gary was Gail's husband and Josh was all of their friend.

When the girl left the salon, she could not wait to tell what she heard at the salon. She called her boyfriend and told him.

Her boyfriend told her not to be involved with the drama because surely someone could get hurt if it ever came out.

The girl agreed but of course, she would not, she wanted to see Sabrina get her ass beat, like most of the girl's in the neighborhood did.

Sabrina saw what she said as a joke but this was very serious to others. Some of the girls that did not see this as funny especially the girls that was married.

They knew if Sabrina could sleep with her best, friend's husband then they did not have a chance when it came to their husband, Sabrina would do him too.

Meanwhile the investigator was hot on Sabrina's trail, he followed her everywhere she went for the day. Keeping notes on her activites, he had a note pad and wrote all she had done on a daily basis.

# The Evidence

The investigator called David after a week of following Sabrina and told David all of Sabrina's activities.

## Day 1
She drove from home to the salon, she was inside for an hour then she came out and drove back home.

## Day 2
She left the house, went to the grocery store, she then drove back home

## Day 3
She drove to her friend Gail house, stayed inside about an hour then left, Gary let her out the house. Before she got off the block, Gail arrived coming from the opposite direction.

## Day 4
She drove to the club, had a drink while talking to the manager. She left the club, got into her truck and returned home.

## Day 5
She worked around the house in the yard.

## Day 6
She stayed inside the house.

## Day 7
She left the house, drove to a man house that name is Josh Strong and she stay inside for an hour and a half. Josh let her out the house, kissing her at the door.She walk to her truck and drove home.

David ask the investigator was he sure she went to Josh house; the investigator told David if he came to his office that he had something to show him.

David agreed to but he asked if the investigator would call Gail so she could be at his office also. The investigator told David "Sure I can call Mrs. Halsey"

David hung the phone up furious, he stormed around the house, talking to himself. "So the motherfucker's are playing me like I am some kind of fool"

In addition, to think I told Josh that I thought Gary was fucking Sabrina when his ass is too. Oh just wait I have something for them both.

Sabrina bitch ass is going to get just what she deserves.

Gary drove to the investigator's office and when he got there, Gail was sitting in the waiting room; David acted surprise to see her.

Hey Gail, how are you? He asks. Gail greeted David and asked if the investigator called him to come in. David said yes in fact he did, he then ask what about you.

Gail reply "yes he did, I wounder what he found out?" David or the investigator never told Gail that David already knew what was going on.

Alternatively, about their conversation on the telephone about Sabrina's activities. David, himself did not know what the investigator had to show them but he was interested in knowing.

The receptionist told David and Gail that they could go into the investigator's office. Gail got up from where she was sitting and David followed.

Gail was nervous but she wanted to know what Gary was doing and with who, David on the other hand was angry and was ready to kick ass.

When they got into the office, they sat down and the investigator pulled out an envelope. He shook the contents of the envelope onto his desk.

The contents were pictures, Gail heart raced as she saw the pictures spill out the envelope because she knew that the pictures possibly contain images that she did not want to see.

David sat up in his chair as the pictures fell out, allowing himself a better view of the images. The investigator picks up the pictures, organizing them together.

He said let us start from the first day that Sabrina was at Gail's house. Gail surprised because she did not know that Sabrina was recently at her house. The investigator pick out a picture, hands it to Gail showing her the entrance to her house. .Then he pick out a picture and hand it to David, it was the picture of Sabrina and Josh.

Gail and David exchange pictures with each other when they were finished looking at them. The room is silent, Gail sniffling and wiping her tear filled eyes.

"Oh David" she yell out, how could they do this to us? David too upset to talk now left the question unanswered. David continues to look through the pictures.

The first pictures were Gary and Sabrina kissing as he walk her out, then the second pictures were Sabrina and Josh together at his house.

David hit the top of the desk as he states, "That whore" next, I will find out that she was fucking the mail carrier.

Gail grap David arm and ask him what they are going to do. David tell her he do not know about her but he want to beat some motherfucker's ass.

The investigator tells David and Gail, you have to use your head in this matter; it is not worth going to jail over or someone getting hurt.

He tells them as hurtful as this is to you, this is what you wanted to find out and the pictures are available for you to use if needed.

David shakes the man hand and he and Gail leave the office. David tell Gail that he want her to go to lunch with him so they could talk about what they were going to do about all this.

Although Gail was upset, she agreed to accompany him to lunch.Gail told David the she would be going to a room after lunch because she did not want her mother to know what was going on.

Gail also told David that she would be moving out of their house because she did not want to see Gary.

At the restaurant, David and Gail sat talking and Gail was crying. David was too angry to be hurt he wanted revenge.

As Gail though about how she and Sabrina were friends so long and for her to do this, she was a snake.

David felt like Josh had played him because all the things that he told him about Sabrina and Gary.

Gail ask David was he going back home, David said "hell yes, that bitch is the one that would be thrown out the house"

He insisted that he paid for the house and Sabrina had to go. Gail told him that he had better not get into any trouble; he told her that he was smarter than that.

Sabrina could not get him to stoop down to her level, That was the last time Gail spoke to David.Sabrina went home and Gary was still gone, she packed her some of her clothing and left.

Gail hurried to a room; she called Michelle and told her what happened. Michelle asked Gail where she was because she wanted to come where she was.

Gail told Michelle and Michelle drove to the room.Michelle told Gail that this is what she trying to warn Gail about all the time.

Gail was very upset; she told Michelle that she felt like killing Sabrina. Michelle told her that she had a right to be upset but to kill someone over this was not woth it.

Michelle assured Gail that she had done the right thing by leaving but what would she say to Gary when he called asking where she was.

Gail said the truth; I will tell him the truth. I will tell him how I had him followed and what I found out. What about Sabrina, what you will do about her, Michelle asked.

Fuck that tramp, David will deal with her. I have nothing to say to her ever again.

However, Gail do not you want to let her know how you feel, Michelle wanted to know. No I do not want to talk to her because she was suppose to be my friend, she know how I feel.

There is nothing I can say to her now for her to know, she is slandalous.

As it was getting late into the day Gail telephone rung, it was Gary asking how long before she would be home.Gail told him that she was at home.

Gary asked what she meant he was at home and she was not there. Gail told Gary how she had him followed and she found out what he was denying to her all the time.

Gary tried to get Gail to come home and they could work this out, Gail told Gary that she did not think so and hung the telephone up.

Back at David house, David waited for Sabrina to come home. Gary got on the telephone to call and warn Sabrina that David might know about them.

Sabrina was in a panick, she did not know what she would do, David was definitely upset and Sabrina was not going home.

Gary told her that Gail told him how Sabrina was fucking him and Josh. Sabrina was surprise that Gary knew it all so now she could not ask him for money for a room because Gary felt Sabrina played him too.

Gary calls Josh and told him that David knew he was fucking Sabrina and he had better stay clear of him.

Josh and Gary talked about how David thought Gary was fucking Sabrina and it came out that he was.

Josh said, "Hey man she was fair game to me and I know you tap that ass too." Gary did not laugh because he was too busy thinking about how he could get Gail to come home.

Gary told Josh but you know what after all this Sabrina was just that a piece of ass. She ruined my marriage, Josh cut Gary off.

No, you ruined your marrige because Sabrina does not owe you nothing she has to explain this to David.and you knew that she and Gail were friends.

Gary interrupts, "yeah but you are friends with David" Josh told him "I was never David friend, I was yours. You introduced me to David and Sabrina.

Josh thought this was funny because he had nothing to lose.Josh been single; he was not obligated to no one. Gary asks "what about Michelle?" Josh asks what about her.

She too was just a piece of ass to me "hell she is not my wife" What can she said to me, Josh ask.

You say that to me but David is not going to look at it this way, he is going to fuck your world around if he sees you.

# Karma

David was tried of waiting for Sabrina, he decided to call her. Sabrina saw the number calling her phone was from her house and she was not about to answer.

David left her a voice mail" bitch when you get this message you will know that I found out about your slutty ass ways"

You had your fun but now is my time, I will see you again and by the way you help your crackhead ass mother pay Scott him money back.

That was when the phone hung up, David was furious now; he could not get to Sabrina to let her know what he thought of her, besides leaving this message.

He knew she heard it but it was not the same as him telling her to her face.

Meanwhile the week had passed and Scott had a hit out for Sabrina mother because she did not give him his money.

There was a knock at her door, she answered it. She opened the door and standing on the outside of it was a man with a ski mask on.

As she opens the door, he began shooting, Sabrina mother got shot three times. Once in the chest and the other times in the face.

She died at the door, the man ran down the hall and into the stairway. After the shooting people came to see what was going on, only to find her lying on the floor in a pool of blood.

Sabrina got to her mother's house and police surrounded it, Sabrina did not know her mother was dead.

One of the neighbors told Sabrina that her mother was
shot, Sabrina panicked and tried to get pass the police
tape. The officer that was guarding the line to make
sure no one was close to the scene stopped her.

Sabrina was yelling but it is my mother! It is my
mother!
The police insisted that she could not go in the
apartment.

The homicide detective came to the line, took Sabrina,
and placed her inside his car. He spoke to Sabrina and
asked her if someone wanted her mother dead.

Sabrina was very upset, she told the detective how her
mother was using drugs and she owed Scott money.

The detective asked Sabrina did she think that she was
in danger too. Sabrina told the detective she did not
trust Scott so she was afraid.

The detective told her that she could go into hiding until
Scott was arrested. Sabrina knew this would be best
because she did not have anywhere to go.

She could not go home David was after her and now
Scott might want her, so she went with the detective.

Sabrina told the detective that she did not have money
to hide anywhere, he assured her that the department
would hide her in a room.Sabrina was happy about this
but she or the detective did not know that the shooter
was watching from the crowd that gathered outside.

The detective told Sabrina that she could not have
contact with no one; he asked if she was married.
Sabrina told him that she was but she and her husband
was separated.

The detective told her that she could not even tell him where she was, Sabrina was not trying to talk to David anyway.

David might do more to her than Scott did if he knew where she was. David was not letting her walk away easy after making a fool of him. Josh on the other hand David wanted to deal with him too, but in his own way.

Sabrina could hide from Scott but she had to come out eventually. Gail continued to stay at the room until she had enough money to find her own house.

Michelle was helping her get her money together to find a house.Michelle was glad that Gail was away from Gary,She did not like Gary anyway she just showed him respect because of Gail

Michelle knew Gary was sneaky and could not be trusted, as she put it all men had to be watched.Gary was not different from the next man when came down to pussy.

Gail told Michelle that she wanted to move to another state, somewhere where Gary would not find her because she was through with him for good.

There were no making up for this; he could never be trusted again. Gail meant this and she stuck to it, Gary would never have her again as his wife. Gail asked Michelle how she could file for a divorce. Michelle told Gail that she would call around and find out.

Michelle was busy looking for divorce laywers, while Gail sat in the room crying about it all. Sabrina was in hiding from David and Scott.

Josh when on with his daily living not worrying about David. Sabrina moved out of state and was not heard from again.

Gail filed her divorce and Gary tried to fight it but it did not work on the grounds of infidelity she was granted the house and monthly alimony from him.

David was shot by a hooker in Cass corrider and now in living in Arizona, never to heard from again.

Scott was arrested for having Sabrina's mother killed and he is serving life in prison without possible chance of parole.

The shooter was never found, who killed Sabrina mother and is free on the street.

Michelle got married and had three children and lives close to Gail in California.

Gail never remarried…But dates often, happily.

Think of the family that is being destroyed by infidelity, if it is you that commits the act, and then remember that life is Karma

What you do will eventually come back to you.

Wheither you believe in karma or not, one day you will know your misfortune was from something you did in your past.

Statistic show that half of all marriages that ended in divorce, infidelity was the number one factor.

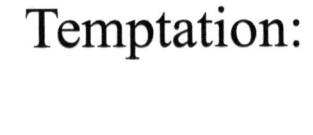

Temptation:

A craving or desire for something,
especially something thought wrong…

The enticing of desire or craving in somebody.

Something that or somebody who tempts
somebody who they know is …

# ~ OFF LIMITS ~

www.ingramcontent.com/pod-product-compliance
Lightning Source LLC
Chambersburg PA
CBHW030342030726
47499CB00003B/871